NO TIME FOR LOVE

Harry was out the door before his pursuer could resurface. Down the stairs three at a time, released the latch, and then was outside and running.

A shot rang out.

Harry flattened himself against the nearest wall, recognizing it as the shooting gallery he'd patronized earlier. Amazing how quickly shooting loses its appeal once you became the target.

Another shot sounded, and without time to consider, Harry vaulted a low wall and landed with a splash.

He was in the Tunnel of Love....

Other Harry Sommers Mysteries by
Peter Whalley
From Avon Books

ROBBERS

Coming Soon

CROOKS

Avon Books are available at special quantity discounts for bulk purchases for sales promotions, premiums, fund raising or educational use. Special books, or book excerpts, can also be created to fit specific needs.

For details write or telephone the office of the Director of Special Markets, Avon Books, Dept. FP, 105 Madison Avenue, New York, New York 10016, 212-481-5653.

ROGUES

PETER WHALLEY

AVON BOOKS NEW YORK

Originally published in Great Britain as *Bandits*.
All the characters and events portrayed in this story are fictitious.

AVON BOOKS
A division of
The Hearst Corporation
105 Madison Avenue
New York, New York 10016

Copyright © 1986 by Peter Whalley
Published by arrangement with Walker Publishing Company, Inc.
Library of Congress Catalog Card Number: 87-22501
ISBN: 0-380-70616-4

All rights reserved, which includes the right to reproduce this book or portions thereof in any form whatsoever except as provided by the U.S. Copyright Law. For information address Walker Publishing Company, Inc., 720 Fifth Avenue, New York, New York 10019.

First Avon Books Printing: September 1989

AVON TRADEMARK REG. U.S. PAT. OFF. AND IN OTHER COUNTRIES, MARCA REGISTRADA, HECHO EN U.S.A.

Printed in the U.S.A.

K-R 10 9 8 7 6 5 4 3 2 1

1

Harry Sommers had been sitting in his parked car for over two hours when the police-car arrived and pulled up behind him. The two policemen in it were both young, clean-shaven and in their shirt-sleeves. They came and stood beside his open window.

'Would you mind getting out of your car a minute, sir?'

'Not at all,' said Harry, and did so.

He'd sensed that they were looking for him the moment their car had turned into the avenue but decided quickly against trying for a quick getaway.

'Do you live round here, sir?'

'No.'

'Well then, would you mind telling us what you're doing here?'

'Do I have to?'

'Well, it would save everybody a lot of time. See, we've had a report that you've been sitting here for most of the morning.'

The second policeman, meanwhile, was reading Harry's number-plate and speaking into his radio, checking that the car wasn't nicked.

'I've been watching that house,' said Harry quietly. He gave a small nod towards a red-brick semi some fifty yards away on the other side of the road.

'And which one would that be, sir?' said the policeman, turning to look. 'Number sixteen?'

'Yes.'

'Funny. That's the lady who rang us with the complaint.'

Harry gave a groan of dismay. So all the time he'd been watching her she'd been looking out at him and wondering what the hell he was doing, stuck there like that on a nice summer morning, leaving his car only to collect an ice-cream. Or perhaps she knew all too well what he was doing and had rung the police as the easiest way of getting rid of him. Either way, it signalled the end of his morning's work.

'And, forgive me asking, but why have you been sitting here all morning watching that house, sir?'

'I'm a private detective,' said Harry.

'Oh, are you now?'

'I've got a card somewhere. . . . ' He had to reach into the car to find one in his discarded jacket.

The policeman took it and studied it.

'Coronet Private Detective Agency . . . ?'

'Yes.'

'Bethnal Green?'

'Yes.'

'Mr Clifford Humphries?'

'Ah, no,' said Harry. 'It's an old card.'

'I see. So what're you watching the house for? Anything we should know about?'

'I doubt it. My client lives there. He's the lady's husband – the lady who rang you about me.'

'What, he wants to know what she gets up to, does he?'

'Something like that.'

'Blimey. Love and marriage, eh.' He handed the card back. 'Still, if it makes work for somebody, it can't be all bad, can it?'

'I suppose not,' said Harry, relieved that they were seeing the funny side of it and didn't seem about to book him for anything.

'Private job, eh. And were you ever in the force?'

Harry shook his head. Not only had he never been a copper: he'd been a fully paid-up member of the other side, always involved with villains of one sort or another and twice doing time in Wormwood Scrubs.

'So how d'you come to be doing a job like this then?' persisted the policeman.

Harry shrugged. 'Answered an advert. Then the bloke I was working for dropped down dead.'

'That a fact? And you took over, did you?'

'More or less.'

The policeman thought about it, and nodded.

'It's an ill wind,' he said contemplatively.

'Listen,' said Harry, 'you won't have to let on to the lady just what I'm doing here, will you? I mean I've made enough of a cock-up of this job as it is. If she finds out her husband's paying good money to have me sitting here then I should think we'll both be in for a bollocking.'

At which they all three shared a chuckle. Harry guessed he'd be joke of the day at the local nick. The bungling amateur. The sleuth who all but gets himself arrested.

'Don't see why we should have to tell her that,' said the policeman. His partner shook his head in agreement. 'Just so long as we can reassure her you're not casing the joint.'

'Cheers,' said Harry, grateful.

They exchanged farewells. He got back in his car and prepared to drive off while the two policemen sauntered over to number 16.

Never mind, he thought. At least it gave him time to go and have a pint. It was too hot for private detectiving. Probably too hot for getting up to a bit of nooky while your husband was at work, come to think of it, so the odds were he'd been wasting his time anyway.

The flat was already less of a mess than it'd been that morning when they'd awoken and both laughed because they hadn't been able to think where they were. And much less of a mess than it'd been yesterday when they'd first moved in.

And at least it was cool down there in the basement of the house. She pushed a lock of blonde hair back into the headscarf she was wearing and paused for an assessment of how much she'd done and how much remained. Everywhere had now been cleaned. It all needed decorating and brightening up of course, but that could come later. What mattered now was to bring order out of chaos. There was still some unpacking to be done, and then all the boxes and crumpled newspapers to be disposed of.

It was difficult, looking round, to think of this as a fresh attempt at sharing her life with a man. It was a new address, certainly, but everything she could see had come from her old one — furniture, pictures, ornaments, books. All he'd brought had been his clothes in two suitcases. It had even made her doubt for a minute. Made her wonder whether she wasn't the one with everything to lose and so the one taking all the risks.

She was certainly the one doing all the cleaning. He, of course, could claim he was working, while she was on holiday and so had the time for it. It was one of the drawbacks of teaching: the holidays were too long to simply waste away; you had to *do* something in them, put them to use.

It would be all right, she told herself. It had to be. She would make sure it was. Never mind that they were as different as chalk and cheese and that it still frightened her to think how much of his life there was that she knew nothing at all about. And didn't want to know about. She was suddenly engulfed by a small panic. No, it wasn't all right. How could it be? She must have been off her head agreeing to move into this dusty dungeon of a flat he'd been so proud of having found because it was in Islington, an area not particularly convenient for either of them but at least equally inconvenient for both. She must have been crazy.

Wild thoughts, that she stilled by making a cup of coffee and going out with it into the small yard that was theirs alone and into which some of the midday sunlight found its way.

Get a grip, she told herself. Remember why you've come here, the real reason for moving. Remember, too, that the man you've come here to be with is kind and considerate — in and out of bed. He doesn't shout or throw things. And he can make you laugh.

She smiled, thinking of the ridiculous way he was impressed by her little learning and how he got upset when she refused to treat her books with all due care and attention. He'd protested as though it were a sacrilege when, on packing to move, she'd tried to throw a load away; she'd had to pretend to rescue them, and wait until he wasn't there before throwing them out again.

The door-bell rang. She wasn't used to its sound and had to think for a moment before recognising it for what it was.

Hurrying to answer its summons, she saw the outline of a man through the frosted glass of the front door and felt a moment of doubt. There was no chain on the door — no time yet for thinking of such things — and she'd had the protection of an entry-phone in her old flat in Chiswick. But, after all, it was the middle of the afternoon, one brightly lit by beguiling sunshine, and whoever was on the other side of the door must have been aware of her approach so she could hardly stop now and refuse to open it.

He stood there, saying nothing. Not needing to say anything.

'Oh no,' she said. 'Oh please God, no.'

With the temperature in the high seventies, the best place to be was the seaside. Like all the other south coast resorts, St Stephen's Bay was enjoying a good season: boarding-houses, parking-spaces, deck-chairs and donkeys were all full.

Not that St Stephen's Bay was everybody's idea of paradise. It couldn't match the razmataz of Brighton up the road or the splendours of Bournemouth; but it did have a couple of miles of presentable promenade, with clean beaches on one side of it and a cheery huddle of pubs, arcades and shops on the other. Radiating outwards from this centre was an abundance of late-Victorian housing, ideal for guest-houses or holiday flats. Some visitors returned each year, liking it because it wasn't Brighton or Bournemouth. It was less formidable, easier to get to know.

There was a single, short pier, as though its builders had been reluctant to advance beyond the shallows. Facing it across the promenade was the Winter Gardens, large and dilapidated. It had once been a ballroom and splendid; now its high windows were boarded over and its roof covered in bird droppings.

Though it wasn't altogether abandoned. Its entrance had been opened up to accommodate an amusement arcade and a fortune-teller's booth, giving the impression that the old and elegant building had been invaded by juvenile squatters. There was a rash of neon signs around the front of the arcade and a dull thump of music coming from within.

Even the good weather didn't deter the punters who, holidaying in search of the sun, now came into the arcade to escape it. The younger end did battle with space invaders and their allies, while their elders and betters fed coins into the one-arm bandits.

'Oh look,' said one of them in surprise, 'it's paying me out and it shouldn't be.'

But her companion wasn't looking. Her machine, too, had started to vomit a stream of coins and she was busy collecting them.

'So's mine.'

So, all of a sudden, was everybody's. There was a steady clattering that grew till it drowned the music as coins were spat out everywhere. At the same time the space invaders had gone berserk and started eliminating one another, and the scores on the pin-ball machines jumped to the hundreds of thousands and then to the millions, promising free games for weeks to come.

The two attendants stared round in dismay.

'What the hell's going on?' said the younger one.

His companion, a middle-aged, bleary-eyed man in charge of the change booth, shook his head: he didn't know either.

Then somebody realised that a single coin put into each of the still silent bandits would start them spewing too and within seconds the whole lot were pumping away, stopping only when their stack of coins was exhausted. People passing outside were drawn in by the clamour and by the excited cries of the players. They scrambled to fill their pockets from the shower of coins; a child's collection of shells was dumped unceremoniously so that its bucket could be used as a scoop; a fight started as two men claimed rights over the same machine.

The young attendant, quicker witted than his mate, shouted, 'We've got to close. Get everybody out!' And he ran to a door in the back of the arcade.

There were a final few seconds of continued madness then everything stopped. The lights snapped off, the machines fell silent and the music came to a sluggish halt. The people, too, stopped their desperate harvesting of coins and looked round guiltily.

'Everybody out please,' called the young man, returning from where he'd thrown the master-switch. 'We're closed.'

Somebody laughed, then everyone was laughing and telling one another how surprised they'd been by the antics of the machines. The two attendants urged and cajoled until finally the arcade was clear and they were able to pull down its steel shutters.

'What in God's name was that all about then?' grunted the older attendant, wiping the sweat from his brow.

'Don't ask me. Bloody things went bananas.'

'Must have been a reason. Reason for everything.'

The young man thought about it, then smiled.

'They always say that machines'll take over one day, don't they? Maybe that was just the beginning.'

Harry returned that evening to a clean and well-ordered flat that was barely recognisable as the same, shambolic place he'd left that morning.

'Marvellous,' he enthused. 'Looks fantastic.'

'And how do I look?' Jill asked, from where she was sprawled across the sofa.

'Oh, you look a wreck. But the flat looks fantastic.'

She laughed. 'Thanks.'

He dropped down beside her and held her chin so as to gaze into her eyes.

'I love you.'

'And I love you. It's just cleaning I can't stand.'

'You want to eat out?'

'You must be joking. After I've spent all day making this place habitable . . . ?'

'I just thought you wouldn't want to cook.'

'Too right I don't. Let's get a take-away.'

'OK.'

'You go and get it while I have a bath.'

But first they had a drink together, opening the bottle of wine he'd bought to celebrate their first full day in the new flat.

He told her about his fiasco of the morning when his surveillance had been brought to an abrupt end by the two policemen.

'I felt a right berk. I mean I'm supposed to be discreet, keep out of sight and all that. Not frighten people into ringing the police to say there's some nutter sitting outside in his car.'

Jill was amused. 'And what were you watching the house for?'

'Oh, her husband seemed to think she might have men-friends calling.'

'And does she?'

'Not that I saw.'

'How do you know it wasn't one of the two policemen?'

'What?' he said in surprise.

'The policemen that moved you on. Couldn't one of them have been her lover?'

Harry looked again into her green eyes, trying to assess how serious she was being. And decided she wasn't being serious at all.

'Don't try and complicate things. It was bad enough as it was. So what about you? What sort of day did you have?'

'Dirty.'

'Oh, I know that. I mean did anybody call? Or anybody telephone?'

'I had a couple of calls from people who'd got my card saying I'd moved. Nothing for you though.'

'I'm not surprised. I haven't told anybody I've moved.'

'Anyway . . .' she stood up '. . . I'm going to get that bath. I'll have a pizza please. With extra chillis.'

'You didn't have any visitors though?' he called after her. 'I mean did you meet any of the other tenants or anything?'

'No,' she said. 'Nobody.'

And she closed the bathroom door.

2

The offices of the Coronet Private Detective Agency were situated above a dry-cleaners in Bethnal Green. Neither a fashionable address nor sumptuous accommodation, it did however allow clients to make a discreet approach with the aid of a bundle of clothing. Another, more important advantage of the location was its low rent. Against which had to be set the main disadvantage, which was the all-pervasive smell of dry-cleaning fluid from below.

Clifford Humphries' will had bequeathed the agency lock, stock and barrel to Yvonne Robinson, his forty-year-old assistant. If most people had been surprised by the provision, Harry had been even more surprised to learn the reason for it: that the owl-eyed, fourteen-stone Yvonne had been Clifford's long-standing mistress.

However, his regard for her had risen steadily since the day she'd talked him into joining her in a desperate attempt at keeping the business afloat. She was a mine of information and knew all there was to know about their strange, nebulous profession. Perhaps Clifford's bequest had been motivated by more than mere affection.

Arriving at the office the following morning, Harry told her about the surveillance fiasco.

'What do you think?' he asked. 'Shall we tell the client what happened?'

Yvonne thought about it.

'You don't know if the wife knew what you were doing. . . ?'

'No. But I can hardly go back very easily.'

'Well, let's wait and see if he gets on to us about it. No point in owning up if we haven't been found out.'

'True.'

'Oh and, before I forget . . .' She consulted her message pad. 'A gentleman called Charlie Monroe rang. He said he was a friend of yours and would you like to meet him for lunch in the Half Moon pub at Covent Garden at one o'clock?'

'Charlie Monroe . . . ?' echoed Harry in surprise.

'Yes. Is he not a friend of yours?'

'Friend of everybody's is Charlie. Or so he likes to think.'

'You sound as though you don't like him.'

'I could never decide. I used to work for him.'

'Well, I think he wants you to work for him again. Wants the agency to anyway.'

'Doing what?'

'He didn't say.'

'Oh well. Can't do any harm to meet him I suppose.'

Five years ago Charlie Monroe had come up from the south coast to try his arm in the big city and with money to burn; he'd formed an unholy alliance with Mickey Baxter, a London villain happy to help him burn it. They'd opened a club in Twickenham, spending a bomb on the décor and on entertaining Mickey's friends from up West. The place had flopped badly and Charlie, able to spot a loser when he found himself riding it, pulled out fast and went back to the seaside.

Harry, bouncer, barman and bottle-washer, had been left jobless and owed a week's wages.

'He didn't say anything about what sort of work it was. . . ?'

'No. Said he'd explain all that when he saw you.'

It'd better be over-and-above board, resolved Harry privately. Better be completely legit. He was now involved in a kosher and respectable business and had to be careful about such things. Besides which, Jill would cut his throat if he wasn't.

By mid-morning the temperature was again in the seventies and still climbing. The beach at St Stephen's Bay was full of sun-worshippers and sand-castle-builders, all edging slowly backward as the tide rolled in. Elsewhere there was a roller-skating competition on the pier, a display of shell-sculpture in the Marine Pavilion and a traffic-jam along the promenade.

The traffic-jam was centred around a huge cement-carrier which had stopped and reversed till it was now halting traffic in both directions. The intention behind this manoeuvre had been to deposit its three-ton load of liquid cement slap-bang in the entrance of the Winter Gardens amusement arcade.

Fortunately Gypsy Rose Lee, the fortune-teller next door, had foreseen what was to come and alerted the arcade's attendants in the nick of time.

They were now on the pavement arguing with the driver of the cement-carrier while around them cars were hooting, and irritable, perspiring drivers were making unhelpful comments through their lowered windows.

'Read my docket,' insisted the driver. 'Does that say Winter Gardens or does that not say Winter Gardens?'

The younger of the two attendants pushed the grimy piece of paper back at him.

'Do we look like a bleeding building-site? I mean what the hell would we want with a load of cement?'

'That's not my problem.'

'I think you've been conned,' said the older of the two attendants. 'Somebody's been taking the piss.'

'Not with me, they're not. Read my docket.'

'We've read your bleeding docket.'

Two traffic-wardens had arrived and were looking on in dismay.

'Can't you move the wagon first and then discuss it?' asked one.

'Easy for you to say that,' said the driver, becoming belligerent. 'Then what the hell am I supposed to do with three tons of liquid cement?'

The younger attendant told him; the driver stepped forward threateningly; the younger attendant, standing six inches taller, put both hands on his chest and gave him a push that sent him slamming back into the front of his wagon. The watching motorists cheered and one of the traffic-wardens radioed for police assistance.

'You saw that,' said the driver to everybody. 'That was assault. Unprovoked assault.'

The motorists cheered again.

'Can't you please move it?' pleaded one of the traffic-wardens.

'No.'

'Listen,' said the younger attendant, grabbing him by the lapels of his overall. 'If you don't move this load of shit right now then I'm going to pick you up and I'm going to drop you head-first straight into it.'

There was a sound of distant police sirens.

'D'you think I should try and get hold of the gaffer?' asked the older attendant.

'No need,' said the younger. He took the docket from the driver's hand and tore it into small pieces.

'That's an offence as well,' said the driver.

'Now you've got no docket, have you?' said the younger attendant. 'So you've got nothing that says you've to leave the shit here.'

'I've got the carbon though, haven't I? I've still got the carbon in the cab.'

Gypsy Rose Lee stepped forward quickly and placed a restraining hand on the driver's arm.

'Come on, love,' she said soothingly. 'I'm sure it's lovely cement but, fact is, you've been given the wrong address.'

'It's never happened before,' said the driver stubbornly.

'We've had a lot of things happen here that've never happened before.'

Unable to get through the packed mass of cars, the police arrived on foot. The driver tried to interest them in the fragments of his docket but they weren't having any of it – he could move his wagon pronto and never mind the legal niceties of the situation. Within ten minutes the cement-carrier had been reversed, the traffic was on the move and the Winter Gardens saved from the threat of having its one-arm bandits incarcerated in cement.

The two arcade attendants wandered back to the change

booth. Gypsy Rose Lee came with them.

'And so what's next?' she said with a gesture of helplessness. 'Just what is the next crazy thing that's going to happen here?'

'Now be fair, Rose,' said the younger attendant. 'You're the one that's supposed to be telling us that.'

Harry turned up at the Half Moon as per Yvonne's arrangements but he couldn't see anybody resembling Charlie Monroe and so settled down to wait, ordering a pie and a pint by way of sustenance. It'll have to be legit, he reminded himself again. Whatever the job is, it'll have to be straight. No more fancy clubs with card games in the back room and tarts operating from the flat upstairs. Those days were gone, and not missed either.

The Half Moon pub had once served the porters of the old Covent Garden market but now, like the market itself, was teeming with the trendy and the youthful. The summer fashions of the women seemed flimsier than ever. Harry realised he didn't mind how late Charlie might be, or even if he didn't come at all.

Then there he was, edging through the groups of drinkers, searching for Harry — Charlie Monroe, as flash as ever and looking not a day older, even, if anything, several days younger, than when Harry had last set eyes on him, which was through the window of his Jaguar as he shouted, 'Be in touch, Harry boy,' and sped off towards the A23 and the seaside. He was wearing a pair of shaded glasses and a light-weight suit over an open-necked cotton shirt. Then, at last, he spotted Harry and it was the big smile and the glad hand.

'Harry boy — and looking better than ever!'

'Hello, Charlie. You're not looking so bad yourself.'

'Well, you have it to do, you know how it is. Large Scotch, darling, please.' This last to the barmaid. 'And what's your poison these days, Harry boy?'

'Another pint'd be very nice.'

'Then another pint it shall be. And what's yours, Derek? The old dicky tum still calling the tune is it?'

And Harry saw for the first time that Charlie wasn't alone but had been followed to the bar by a small, stocky man some years his senior.

'Still got to watch it, yes,' he said, with a smile that included Harry. 'Keep the old ulcer happy. Tomato juice is about my limit.'

'Tomato juice,' said Charlie. 'And let me introduce you two. Harry Sommers, this is Derek Underhill, friend of mine from down South.'

They shook hands. Harry thought Derek Underhill, with his nodding and smiling, seemed a touch over-awed, though whether it was by the trendy surroundings of the Half Moon or the overpowering geniality of Charlie Monroe he couldn't have said. All that was certain was that Underhill was somewhere in his fifties, had thinning grey hair and watery blue eyes.

'And how long have you been in this private eye line of business then?' enquired Charlie as they waited for their drinks to be served.

'Oh, not long,' said Harry, then realised it was coming up for the best part of a year. How time flew when you were struggling to survive.

'I heard from Mickey Baxter it was what you was doing. You remember Mickey and the club that him and me used to run?' He turned to Underhill. 'Like I was telling you, Harry here was a regular part of the team back in them days.'

'I'm still short of a week's wages on that,' said Harry.

Charlie laughed. 'You and me both. Only more like a year's wages in my case.'

'So what're you up to nowadays?' asked Harry.

'Oh, same as ever. Bit of this, bit of that.'

'You still down in Brighton or wherever it is?'

'St Stephen's Bay,' Charlie corrected him.

'Better than Brighton,' added Underhill with a smile.

'Well, let's be honest, Derek,' said Charlie. 'It might not be better but at least the rates are lower. Yes, I'm sticking strictly to the coast these days, Harry. Doing what I know about. No more adventures in the big city. Once bitten, twice shy — you know how it is.'

'So what brings you up here today then?' asked Harry, feeling it was time to move from the jolly banter to the point and purpose of their meeting.

'Oh, I'm not averse to the odd bit of visiting. In fact I've got a little flat up here. Gives the missus somewhere to do her shopping from.'

'But you wanted to see me about some business?'

'Well, that's as may be, but there's no hurry is there? I mean first of all let me tell you something about Derek here, all right?'

'Sure.'

'Not much to tell,' said Underhill.

'See, Derek and me, we're in what you might call the same trade. The holiday trade. And in the same resort. That's St Stephen's Bay of course. And as such we've had a professional and social acquaintance going back many years.'

'I remember Charlie when he was as poor as I am now,' said Underhill.

'I was never as poor as what you are now,' said Charlie, beaming. To remind him of his money was the greatest compliment you could pay him.

'That's true, is that.'

Harry found himself beginning to warm to Underhill. More anyway than he'd ever warmed to Charlie Monroe who, for all his back-slapping bonhomie, was about as convivial as a polar-bear.

'Anyhow,' said Charlie, getting back to his explanation, 'I have the fairground and a few caffs and some other interests around the resort. So I'm sort of what you might call diversified. While Derek here's always stuck to the machines.'

'One-arm bandits,' said Derek, for Harry's benefit. 'I have this arcade. It's only the one arcade. Nothing like the sort of operation he has.'

Charlie laughed, pleased to have it brought to Harry's attention just what a big cheese he was down there among the seagulls. He might have come a cropper on his one incursion into the metropolis but he'd had his backside well covered.

He could even afford a word of encouragement for his small-time colleague.

'Well, it's not as small as all that, Derek boy. I mean, be honest, you have got just about the biggest building in the whole town.'

Underhill pulled a face. 'For what good it does me.'

'Winter Gardens,' said Charlie to Harry. 'D'you know it?'

Harry shook his head. 'I don't think I've ever been to St Stephen's Bay, sorry and all that.'

'You're not missing much,' said Underhill.

'He's got the biggest building in the whole town,' repeated Charlie. 'If there's ever another war he'll be on to a fortune. It's the only place on the south coast big enough for keeping airships.'

And he laughed. Derek Underhill's small smile suggested he might well have heard the line before.

'It's just an arcade,' he said.

'Well, look then,' said Charlie, 'now that I've done my duty in bringing you two together, I think I'll just leave you to it and go and sort out a bit of business that I've got.'

'It's not you that's got the work for me then?' asked Harry in surprise.

'No, it's him.'

'It's me,' said Underhill. 'Only it had to be somebody from out of town — out of St Stephen's Bay that is — so I asked Charlie here if he knew of anybody suitable.'

'Suitable for what?' asked Harry cautiously.

But he didn't get his answer until there'd been a round of handshaking and promises to keep in touch and Charlie had finally left them. Derek Underhill bought another round, which they took outside to where there were some tables.

'I've been having some bother in the arcade,' he said.

'What sort of bother?'

'Strange things happening. It looks like somebody's trying to sabotage the whole operation and put me out of business. So what I need is somebody that'll find out what's going on and who's behind it.'

Doesn't sound like one for me then, thought Harry, though he could well understand why Charlie Monroe had recommended him – remembering him only as hired muscle who knew how to look after himself and his employer's premises and no doubt thinking him still in much the same line of work. Still, there was no harm in listening.

'What sort of things have they been up to?'

'Oh, little things to start with. For instance, we turned up one morning and found the locks had got that super-glue in 'em. Well, that took some getting rid of, I can tell you. Then we've had stink-bombs left all around the place so that the punters step on 'em and then it's hold your nose and everybody head for the door.'

All sounds a bit petty, thought Harry. 'Has anybody been round offering protection?'

'Nobody. All there's been is all kinds of weird things being delivered. Like one day we had two hundred non-stick frying-pans, then another day it was cricket-bats. Oh, and then a goat – some farmer coming in with this goat that he swore we'd ordered from him. Well, I mean, some people might think that's funny but me, I stopped laughing some time ago, you know what I mean?'

'Yes,' said Harry, managing to keep a straight face.

'And there've been other things. Letters written to the council about us – one saying I'm using the place to sell porno-videos – so that I have all kinds of nosey-parkers coming in and poking around. And like as not setting off the odd undiscovered stink-bomb in the process. I tell you, it's getting me down. And it's getting the lads down an' all.'

'I can imagine.'

'Height of the season as well you see. I can't afford this kind of hassle anytime, least of all now. And I haven't told you the best one yet.'

'What's that?'

'What happened the other day. Somebody got into the back of the arcade and tampered with the electrics. Just made it so the supply to the machines was less than it ought to have been. And the result is they go bananas. The bandits start paying out like there's no tomorrow, the videos go into overdrive and the whole place is like some kind of mad house.'

Harry laughed; he couldn't help it.

Derek Underhill nodded and gave a wry smile. 'I know. Sounds like a bundle of laughs when you're hearing about it.' And he drained his tomato juice.

'Let me get you another one, eh?' said Harry. 'What is it, same again?'

Derek Underhill considered a moment, then said, 'A scotch-and-water would be better. What the doc never knows can't hurt him, can it?'

So Harry brought him a scotch-and-water and then settled again in the sunshine to hear the remainder of the story. He felt sorry for Underhill, who seemed a decent enough bloke, desperate for someone to turn to. Though that didn't mean that Harry was going to put himself in the firing-line. The agency was ticking over nicely; he'd just moved into the new flat with Jill; it was a sunny day in London town. Why the hell should he want to get entangled in a load of south coast aggro?

'Cheers,' said Underhill, sipping his drink, and then went on: 'Anyhow, it's time it was put a stop to. Before I go round the twist and probably out of business as well. Which is why I went to Charlie and I said, "Charlie, do you know anybody that might be able to sort out this mess?" And he says, "Let me have a think," and then, when he's had his think, he comes back and tells me about yourself.'

'Have you been to the police?' asked Harry avoiding having to respond to that.

Derek Underhill gave a snort of contempt. 'You're joking.'

'Well, why not? I mean if you think it's getting serious . . . ?'

'The police have no time for us. You ask Charlie about that if you don't believe me. You could be running an arcade and have people murdering one another and you could ring the police and you wouldn't see so much as a panda-car till the day after tomorrow. See, they don't like the business we're in. They think we're

a load of crooks.'

Harry nodded, recognising the complaint. It was a familiar grievance among those whose occupations veered towards the seamy side: that any problems they had were their own; nobody wanted to know. Massage parlours, snooker halls, doss houses, gaming clubs . . . along with amusement arcades, they were a twilight world in which they were expected to sort out their own bother without help from the local fuzz.

'Which was why I thought a private detective might be best.'

Harry demurred. 'I don't see there's a lot I could do.'

'Well, what I thought — if you could come down and work in the arcade for a week or two. Sort of undercover. Keep your eyes and ears open and see what you might pick up. For one thing, how do I know it's not somebody on my staff that's behind it?'

'It's not the sort of work I normally do.'

'Well, no. I didn't imagine it would be. But Charlie said you was the man for the job.'

Harry hesitated. Perhaps he should consider it. Or at least not reject it out-of-hand: there wasn't all that much work about. Though tracking down the mysterious saboteur of St Stephen's Bay sounded well outside his normal scope of process-serving, surveillance and missing persons.

'But I don't know the first thing about working in an arcade.'

'What is there to know? And you won't be on your own. There'll always be somebody else there with you.'

'And suppose they find out what I'm doing there?'

'They won't. We'll just say you're temporary relief while I'm going to be off for a week or two.'

Harry had the strange sensation that, rather than talking the other man out of the idea, he was succeeding only in talking himself further into it.

'But suppose . . . suppose I don't find out anything? That'll make me a very pricey way of getting your temporary relief.'

'So let me do the worrying about that. And you need have no doubts over the money. I can put that up in advance if you like. And of course there'll be accommodation provided. All expenses.'

'Why not get somebody local, somebody that knows the patch?'

"Cause if he knows the patch then my lads are going to know him. Which is why I asked Charlie to recommend somebody.'

Harry grasped at a final straw.

'The real problem is what would happen to my business if I was to be away for that length of time. So I mean I can't give you an answer now anyway. I'll have to talk to my associate about it.'

'Fair enough,' said Derek Underhill. 'I can see that. Well look, shall I give you my number and perhaps you can give me a ring tonight or tomorrow to say if you're interested?'

'Sure,' said Harry, taking the card the other man was offering.

'Then we can talk money and all the rest of it after that.'

'I mean – touch wood – the aggro might have stopped by then anyway.'

'Might have got worse as well.' He clutched his stomach and gave a small burp. 'Shouldn't have had that scotch. Still, we're none of us going to live forever, are we?'

Surprisingly, Yvonne didn't mind one bit the idea of his leaving her to hold the fort while he disappeared to St Stephen's Bay. In fact, it tied in most conveniently with her new-found determination to get out and about more often.

'I can handle any process-serving that comes along,' she reassured him. 'There was a time I always used to do it when Clifford was otherwise occupied. Before he took you on.'

'It might be for as long as two weeks though.'

'I'm sure I can manage.' She was beginning to sound offended.

'I'm sure you can. I just didn't know whether you'd want to.'

'I don't mind. I was thinking about that surveillance case — the one where she called the police.'

'Yes,' said Harry, remembering all too well.

'I think I should take that over for a start. There's no way you can go down that avenue again, is there?'

'Not really,' admitted Harry.

'And this other job sounds as though it'll pay well. Not the sort we should be turning down if you ask me.'

Even more surprisingly, Jill saw no objections either. She'd spent the day painting the kitchen; he got back to find her out in the yard, relaxing with a cup of coffee and a copy of Graham Greene's *The Heart of the Matter* which he knew she had to teach next term as part of the A-level English course. He got himself a coffee and a chair and joined her. He explained about his lunchtime meeting with Derek Underhill and the offer of work it had led to. He spoke lightly, as if the whole thing were as much a joke as something to be contemplated seriously.

'And so are you going?'

'Oh . . . I doubt it.'

'Why?'

'Well, only just moved in here, haven't we? I want to help you get this place ship-shape, not leave you to do it all by yourself.'

'I haven't noticed you helping much.'

'I've been working.'

'So? Go and work down in Brighton or wherever it is.'

'St Stephen's Bay.'

'St Stephen's Bay.'

He looked at her, wondering whether she was teasing. Even after their months together, he was never sure.

'I'll tell you what,' she said. 'You go, and leave me to work on this dump for a couple of days. Then I'll come down and join you. We'll have a holiday.'

He hesitated. 'I'll be undercover.'

She roared with laughter at the espionage jargon. 'You'll be what. . . ?'

'I mean,' he said patiently, 'no-one else will know what I'm doing there.'

'So I'll be undercover as well. We'll pretend I'm some bird you've picked up on the pier. I'll call myself Cindy and paint my nails turquoise.'

'Listen,' he said, feeling under pressure, 'I don't even know if I want the bloody job. Either it'll be kids messing about — in which case I'll be wasting my time — or it'll be some sort of protection racket — in which case I'll be landing myself with a lot of bother.'

And that, he thought, was sure to deter her. Normally the slightest hint of violence was sufficient to remind her of his villainous past and start her pleading with him to keep well away from anything that might take him back to it.

But now all she said was: 'I can't believe there's anything very terrible goes on in St Stephen's Bay. It's not exactly Soho, is it?'

'I don't suppose it is.'

'Super-glue and stink-bombs. Sounds more like the sort of thing we get at school.'

He was beginning to get the distinct impression she actually wanted him out of the way. Though it seemed hardly possible to suspect her of an ulterior motive. Not two days after she'd taken the brave, even foolhardy step of moving into the new flat with him.

He shrugged. 'You're probably right.'

'So you'll go?'

'I'll think about it.'

It was a bizarre job — undercover agent in the land of one-arm bandits and pin-ball machines. Clifford Humphries, his erstwhile employer, would probably have rejected it without a second thought; part of Harry still insisted he should do the same.

On the other hand, a week or two at the seaside wasn't to be sniffed at, particularly if Jill meant what she said about joining him. It'd be their first holiday together. They'd stroll arm-in-arm along the prom and have their picture taken doing so, evidence of happy times to keep against an uncertain future.

It'd been a long, hard day for the two attendants at the Winter Gardens amusement arcade. On top of the unscheduled arrival of the cement-carrier, there'd been the absence of the boss — up in London on some business or other — which had meant them working through without relief until ten o'clock when at last they could pull down the steel shutters. Gypsy Rose Lee was long gone, her booth dark and deserted.

'Coming for a drink then?' asked the older attendant.

'Not yet,' said the younger. 'Might catch up with you later.'

'You seeing some bird? On a promise, are you?'

'I'm the one that makes the promises,' said the young man with a wink. 'Cheers now.' And he strode quickly away.

The older man called, 'See you, Nick,' and headed for the Grand Hotel where he was so well-known as to be considered an honorary resident when it came to the ticklish question of late-night drinking.

The younger attendant increased his pace till he was jogging along the promenade, side-stepping between the strolling couples and the families out late with crying children. Many of the places he passed were still open, selling fish and chips, sticks of rock, printed T-shirts, pizzas and souvenirs of all shapes and sizes. The heavy beat of a disco came from Davy Jones' Locker (previously the Crystal Rooms) and there was a late-night cabaret at the Carleton Club. The string of coloured lights above him was hardly needed, so bright was the moon.

He came to the fairground, which was itself in the act of closing and whose customers were drifting out to join the throng on the promenade. He stood for a moment at the side of the main entrance, peering in at the near-deserted site as though looking for somebody who might have lingered.

Then, apparently satisfied, he turned away, darted between the crawling traffic and hurried to a telephone-kiosk on the other side of the promenade. He dialled a number and waited. He seemed anxious as he did so, then his frown cleared, he spoke into the mouthpiece and listened to the reply.

He put down the receiver and came out of the kiosk, back into the warm night air and the good-natured crowds. He began to run again, now going away from the gaudy centre and heading for the quieter suburbs.

3

The train carrying Harry south was electric and clean and new. Only its air-conditioning seemed less than perfect so that the air inside the carriages was hot and heavy. Passengers made fans out of newspapers and fondly remembered a time when air-conditioning was unknown and windows made to open.

It was two days since Harry's meeting with Derek Underhill and no more than twenty-four hours since he'd rung him to say, yes, he'd take the job. Underhill had been enthusiastic and grateful and raised no objections about the fee, which was somewhat in excess of the agency's usual.

Yvonne was to run things in his absence and seemed unperturbed by the prospect.

Jill, too, seemed to think she could get on better without him, at least as far as the decorating was concerned. She came with him to Victoria Station to say goodbye.

'I've bought you a present,' she said, pulling a paperback book from her pocket. 'Give you something to read on the way down.'

It was a copy of *Brighton Rock* by Graham Greene.

'Well, thanks,' he said, turning it over in his hands.

'I thought it might be appropriate. It's about seaside gangs and murders.'

'Then I hope it's not appropriate.'

She smiled. 'Oh, don't worry. I'll soon be down to keep an eye on you.'

For Harry had taken up her suggestion that she should come down and join him. When he'd been wondering whether he really wanted such an extraordinary and out-of-the-way commission, it was the thought of the two of them strolling together along the promenade that'd tipped the scales. She was to give him three days to settle in and then — he'd made her solemnly promise — she was going to pack her bags and follow him. It was a nice feeling, that this wasn't really a job at all but an expenses-paid holiday in return for which he couldn't see himself being called upon to do much more than stand around a slot-machine arcade for a few hours a day and dish out change to snotty kids.

At least it would be cooler by the sea. He tried to concentrate on his book. Between short dozes and distracting glimpses of the passing world outside, he got a confused impression of a story about a man called Hale who visited Brighton on a hot summer's day and was murdered. He didn't get far enough to discover who'd murdered him or why. What struck him was the comparison between this character Hale and himself. Here he was travelling incognito to St Stephen's Bay while, in the book, Hale had been travelling incognito around Brighton. It wasn't an exact parallel of course, just the odd points of similarity: the south coast resort, the summer's day, the undercover role.

Either it was Jill's little joke or she hadn't realised. Either way he wasn't going to let it bother him. His own investigation was small fry compared to this murky tale of casual slaughter.

Before he had the chance to read on, they were arriving, with platform signs saying 'St Stephen's Bay' sliding ever more slowly past the window. He thrust the book into his pocket and waited his turn to alight.

Derek Underhill was waiting at the ticket-barrier, pleased to see him. He led him out into the station forecourt where he stowed Harry's suitcase in the boot of his Rover 3·5.

'There's a lot of people get the wrong idea about this business,' he said, climbing into the driving-seat. 'They think anybody who has an arcade must be rich. Well, look at me. I have one and I'm not. I'll tell you what the trouble is, shall I? People go into clubs and they see machines there that can pay out jackpots of up to one hundred pounds at a time. And they see the sorts of profits these machines are making for these clubs. And they look at all the machines I've got and they say — by Christ, the man who owns this lot must be rich.'

'I suppose so,' said Harry, catching his first glimpse of the sea. He surprised himself, feeling his spirits lift at the sight of the beach with all its gaudy paraphernalia. He'd never been to St Stephen's Bay before in his life yet everything he now saw of it was nostalgic and reassuring. There was something from childhood here that'd never gone away.

'But we aren't allowed that kind of machine,' went on Derek. 'Ours have a top limit payout of one-fifty in cash or three pounds in tokens. So straightaway you can see we're talking about very different percentages.'

Harry nodded, keeping up a show of interest, though really bemused and intoxicated by all they were passing. You forgot about all this when you didn't have kids of your own. The sandcastle-building, the ice-creams and the donkey-rides. Yet here it all was, nothing changed.

'And then it's a short season. I mean, we're open all year right enough, but the place only fills up in May and then by the end of September it's as dead as a dodo so you don't have much time to make any real money.'

Harry gave a grunt of agreement, though he didn't believe much of what he was hearing. He knew a little about the London arcades and the kind of money they turned over. Here might have been a bit different but not enough to have Derek Underhill crying poverty.

'And then there's the VAT we pay. And I do mean that *we* pay, not the punters. 'Cause there's no way you can put fifteen per cent on the coin that somebody's putting into a machine. And then there's the Betting and Gaming Permit we have to have. It's amazing there's still so many in business.'

'It is,' said Harry, looking at the packed acres of flesh. There was a Punch-and-Judy show, too, with an attentive audience of children in front of it.

'And don't forget what I told you about the police. They just do not want to know. As far as they're concerned we might just as well be a bunch of crooks ourselves. Which we're not of course.

As everybody that knows us will testify.' He lifted a hand from the steering-wheel and pointed. 'There it is, there. That's me.'

Harry looked along the frontage of shops and pubs and arcades and saw the words 'Winter Gardens' on a building that rose above the others.

Feeling that something complimentary was called for, he said, 'Quite some building. And right in the centre of things too.'

'Right in the centre of an old ruin,' said Derek. 'That's what I am. I should be paid by the government for keeping that place going. I'm doing a public service.'

As they drew nearer, Harry saw it was, indeed, a monster, every bit as big as Charlie Monroe had described it. You could see from the decorative stonework, now chipped and gap-toothed, that it must once have had pretensions. Derek didn't stop and they passed by on the other side of the road. Harry caught a glimpse of the dark interior of the arcade but could make out nothing more before they'd left it behind.

'I thought I'd take you to your digs first,' said Derek. 'Let you get yourself established.'

'Fine,' said Harry. Then asked, 'There's nothing else happened since we spoke, has there?'

'Not since yesterday, no. But there was something while I was up in London seeing you.'

Harry waited. Derek's concentration had gone to his driving, nudging his way through the opposing stream of traffic to take them off the promenade and down an avenue of tall semis. Each had its own display of signs in the front window: 'Seaview', 'Bed and Breakfast', 'No Vacancies', 'Peacehaven', 'Hot and Cold in All Bedrooms', 'No Vacancies', 'Colour Television', 'Taj Mahal', 'Private Facilities', 'No Vacancies'.

'Somebody rang and ordered three tons of liquid cement for the arcade. And some idiot of a driver tried to deliver it.'

'I hope somebody managed to stop him,' said Harry, suppressing a grin.

'Only just.'

They stopped. 'Floribunda,' said the signs. 'Bed and Breakfast', 'Sorry No Pets', 'No Vacancies'.

'I hope this is to your liking,' said Derek. 'Only I was a bit pushed to find anywhere this time in the season. And I couldn't put you in a hotel in case that'd give the game away.'

'I don't have to use a false name or anything, do I?' asked Harry uneasily. Such misgivings about the job as remained were centred around the notion of acting a part, pretending to be somebody he wasn't.

'I don't see why,' said Derek. 'So long as they don't know the real reason you're here, it doesn't matter what they think your name is, does it?'

They came into a small hallway where everything was spick and span and smelt of polish. There was a collection of brochures and posters grouped on a notice-board and, below them, a small brass gong.

'Anybody at home?' called Derek.

There were footsteps coming from below, and then a brisk, young woman appeared wearing an apron and a fixed, welcoming smile.

'Hello. I'm Mrs Melling. Can I help you?'

Derek explained who Harry was and reminded her of the reservation he'd made earlier. Mrs Melling smiled and nodded and took a small card from a drawer in the hall table.

'Would you fill that in please?' she asked, handing it to Harry.

He entered his name and address, remembering in time to use his new home address and not that of the agency.

'No point in me hanging about here,' said Derek. 'You think you can find your own way back to the arcade, do you?'

'No problem,' said Harry.

'Right. Well then I'll see you there in about half-an-hour, OK?'

And he left Harry to the tender mercies of Mrs Melling, who looked at his completed card and said, 'Thank you. This way please.'

He picked up his suitcase and followed her up the twisting stairs to what he knew, even as he set foot on the first step, was going to be the top floor. She indicated the bathroom and toilets as they passed them and then abandoned him to ascend the final two flights alone.

'It's the room at the very top of the stairs. Breakfast is between seven-thirty and nine o'clock, and tea or coffee can be ordered in the lounge between eight and ten-thirty in the evening. I hope you'll find everything to your satisfaction.'

What Harry found was an attic room, slightly larger than he'd expected and with the usual arrangement of bed, wardrobe and dressing-table. There was a wash-basin with a single glass upended on the shelf above it.

Home for two weeks then. Could be worse, he thought, pushing the window open and hearing the cries of the seagulls. Could be a hell of a sight worse, in fact. He'd had smaller rooms than this. Rooms with bars across the windows. Rooms with no windows at all. Though, thinking about it, he had to admit he'd probably never had one that was higher.

It took him no more than five minutes to unpack his suitcase, have a wash and then descend again past the other, deserted bedrooms and the signs saying 'No Smoking' and 'Consider Others'. He was in no hurry, strolling towards the Winter Gardens at a leisurely pace that would give Derek Underhill time to get there before him. He felt himself on holiday, no doubt about it; he stopped to breathe deeply and savour the sea air.

'And here he is,' called Derek as he reached the entrance to the Winter Gardens arcade.

Harry nodded and raised a hand in acknowledgement, then advanced to where Derek was standing with two other men whose jackets, with the name 'Winter Gardens' embossed on the breast pockets, identified them as attendants.

'Glad you could make it, Harry,' said Derek, holding out a hand.

'So am I,' said Harry, feeling ridiculous. It was part of their cover-story that they shouldn't already have met that day.

'Now like I told you, boys,' said Derek, turning to the other two, 'Harry here is a friend from way back. And he's going to fill in for a couple of weeks while I follow doctor's orders and get the old feet up.' This was also part of their cover-story. As Derek had observed: 'What's the point in having lousy guts if you can't make 'em work for you sometimes.' He completed the introductions: 'Harry, this is Nick Wyatt' — Nick being the younger of the two — 'and this is Reg Smith' — Reg being the older by some thirty years or more.

'And now let me introduce you to somebody else who's part of the family,' said Derek, leading Harry away. Nick and Reg stood watching him go. Had they been hostile and suspicious or had he imagined it? But Derek was talking. 'This lady is one of the institutions of St Stephen's Bay. Which is probably why I can't bring myself to charge her more than the miniscule rent I get off her now. Hello, Rose darling, are you in?' he called, stepping into the fortune-teller's booth that stood adjacent to the arcade, tucked in beside it under the lee of the decaying frontage.

The woman who emerged may or may not have been a genuine gypsy but certainly looked the part. She wore a headscarf and large, brassy ear-rings. Harry would have put her in her forties, though she might have been a well-preserved sixty, had anyone had the temerity to ask.

'And so this is our new man, is it?' she said, looking Harry up and down.

'That's right, Rose. This is Harry.'

'Well,' she said, 'at least he's better looking than the old one.'

Derek turned to Harry with a gesture of mock-dismay. 'You see the respect I get? Is it any wonder I'm a sick man?'

Rose ignored him. 'And so, where are you from, Harry?' she asked.

'London.'

'East End?'

'Definitely. And where're you from then?' countered Harry as Derek stood patiently waiting.

'I'm a traveller,' she said. 'I don't come from anywhere.'

'It's a while since you've done much travelling, Rose,' said Derek. ''Less you count going to Regent Street for your Christmas shopping.'

They were interrupted by Reg, the older of the two attendants, who stuck his head in through the booth door.

'You got a minute, boss? There's a man here wants a word.'

'Can't you or Nick deal with him?'

'Not really.'

'Why? What's so special about him?'

'He's an undertaker.' There was a moment when no-one spoke. Reg nodded emphatically, then repeated, 'Undertaker. Says he's come to collect a body.'

Derek muttered a single obscenity and, needing no more urging, hurried out after Reg. Rose said, 'This I have to see to believe. . . !' and went out after them, leaving Harry to follow in her wake.

There was a hearse drawn up on the double-yellow lines outside the arcade. Two men dressed in black suits and ties had come from it and were standing in the midst of the one-arm bandits. Nick, arms folded, stood confronting them.

'What's all this then?' demanded Derek.

'This is Mr Underhill,' said Nick to the undertakers. 'He's the gaffer.'

'Is this number sixty-two to sixty-eight Marine Parade?' enquired one of them.

'Yes,' said Derek. 'So who're you?'

'Oh dear,' said the undertaker, exchanging a glance with his colleague, 'I'm afraid there might have been some kind of mistake.'

'Tell us about it,' said Derek. 'We're getting used to them.'

'We're from the Cooperative Funeral Service. We've come in response to a telephone-call instructing us that our professional services were needed at this address.'

'You mean it said somebody had, er . . . ?'

The undertaker nodded. 'That somebody had passed away, yes.'

32

'Sounds like chummy up to his old tricks again,' said Reg.

'I'd say so,' agreed Nick.

'I know what it sounds like,' snapped Derek. He turned to the undertaker. 'Well, and can you not see what sort of place this is? This is an arcade, right? Not an old people's home. If anybody ever dropped down dead in here – which, touch wood, they haven't done yet – then it'd be an ambulance we'd be after, not you.'

'I can see that now,' said the undertaker. 'Of course. But all we were given was the address. We didn't know what the premises were till we arrived.'

'And then there always might have been a flat upstairs,' added his colleague, sounding resentful.

'And who was it rang you?' said Derek. 'I don't suppose they left a name, did they?'

'Only the name of the deceased.'

'And what was that?'

'Sommers. A Mr Harry Sommers.'

All eyes turned to Harry, who up to this point had been taking a detached observer's interest in the proceedings, but who was now suddenly open-mouthed in astonishment.

'This is Mr Sommers,' said Derek. 'Does he look as though he needs your professional services?'

'Oh dear,' said the undertaker. 'There really has been a mistake, hasn't there?'

'I hope so,' muttered Harry.

'Come on, out,' said Derek. 'And you can get that butcher's van of yours shifted as well. It's not doing my business a lot of good parked out there.'

'Are you all right, love?' said Rose to Harry as the undertakers removed themselves and their hearse. 'Only you look a bit white.'

He managed a laugh. 'I feel a bit white.'

'I wouldn't take any notice. It's just some joker. We've been having this sort of thing for weeks.'

Though he knew that to be true, it didn't make the timing and

33

nature of this latest joke any the less unnerving. He'd barely been in the place for ten minutes, yet here was a morbid prank aimed not just at the arcade as the others had been, but one that had arrived addressed to him personally. Whoever was behind it was uncomfortably well informed.

Derek led him to the small office that was tacked on to the back of the arcade and made both of them a cup of tea. He was full of apologies for the rude nature of Harry's welcome and anxious to find how he'd taken it.

'I can't think how they'd got your name. I can't honestly.'

'Who knew I was coming today?'

'Nobody. Not a soul. Well, apart from me.'

'What about the other three in there?'

'What, Nick, Reg and Rosie? Well, they knew there was this geezer from London coming to stand in for a couple of weeks. And I suppose I might have mentioned your name; I'm not sure now.'

'And Charlie Monroe,' said Harry as the thought struck him.

'Charlie?'

'He knew I was coming.'

'Well, yes, I suppose he did. I can't see anybody having got your name from Charlie though. Mind you, I can't see who the hell they can have got it from. It's not, er . . . it's not put you off, has it?'

'I'm not thinking of getting the next train back if that's what you mean,' said Harry.

Derek gave a sigh of relief. 'That's the spirit. Charlie said you weren't a quitter. He said you were the man for the job.'

Well thanks, thought Harry. He could have done without the notion that his reputation had gone ahead of him. The trouble with being known as a hard man is that there's always somebody who thinks otherwise. This was supposed to have been an easy option, an expenses-paid holiday, and now suddenly it wasn't. The undertakers might have gone but they'd left Harry with the disquieting impression that there might be a nasty side to this job after all.

'Well, time I was off I think,' said Derek eventually. 'I'll leave you in the capable hands of Nick and Reg out there. Actually Nick's the one to listen to. He's a very good lad, very reliable. Not that Reg is unreliable. Just that with one thing and another — mostly pints of bitter — he's not always on the ball isn't old Reg. And you've got my number, have you?' Harry nodded. 'Then I'll wait to hear from you. And what else can I say except — the very best of luck.'

'Thank you,' said Harry.

They came out of the office and into the arcade where it was back to business as usual.

'You'll show Harry what's what, won't you, Nick?' said Derek. 'I'm off to put my feet up for two weeks.'

'Some people have all the luck,' said Nick.

'Some people deserve it.' Turning to Harry, Derek said, 'And thanks for helping me out, Harry. Much appreciated.'

They shook hands and he walked out of the arcade and into the sunshine.

Nick and Reg neither moved nor said anything. Once more Harry felt their hostility, though the reason for it he couldn't yet understand. Did they resent him for the arrival of the undertakers, feeling that, as the victim of the prank, he'd somehow also been responsible for it?

'Well,' he said, trying to sound casual, 'I suppose I'd better make a start then.'

'Suppose so,' said Nick.

But neither seemed inclined to instruct him as to where this start might best be made.

'So what do you want me to do?' he said, becoming exasperated by the lengthening silence. 'Anything in particular?'

'Yes, there is one thing as a matter of fact.'

'And what's that?'

'Why don't you tell us what you're really doing here?'

'What?'

He saw that Gypsy Rose had come from her booth and now came and stood beside the other two.

'We know what your game is, love,' she said.

'Oh yes?' said Harry. 'And so what is it?'

'You're a private detective,' said Nick.

'Private what . . . ?' said Harry with an attempt at a laugh.

'Detective.'

'Come on . . . ! You mean me? A private detective? And where the hell have you got that crazy idea from? Who says I am?'

'I do,' said Nick.

'And me,' said Reg.

'And I've got to agree with the two of them,' said Rose.

4

Perhaps it shouldn't have been such a surprise. Perhaps he should have expected somebody to guess that his arrival had more to do with the problems besetting the arcade than with Derek Underhill's dickey tummy. Perhaps any number of things. What was certain was that his cover was blown before he'd so much as started.

Faced by the three of them, he'd little choice but to own up.

'All right? So what if I am a private detective? Seems like you might need one from what I've been hearing.'

'To check on us?' said Nick. 'No, thank you.'

Ah yes, thought Harry. That's why they aren't too happy about the idea. Sneaking somebody in undercover doesn't exactly add up to a vote of confidence in your own staff.

'It's not to check on you. Just that Mr Underhill thought I might be less . . .' — what was the word? — 'less conspicuous if I came in as casual labour.'

'Looks like he was wrong then, doesn't it?'

'Look at it from our point of view, love,' said Rose. 'How would you like it?'

He thought of calling it a day there and then and catching the next train home. First the undertakers and now this. It wasn't the most auspicious start to a case.

'Look, I can understand you don't like the way this has been set up. But I'm here now anyway. So there's no reason why we can't all work together on the same side, is there?'

'No reason why we should either,' retorted Nick.

It was an attitude that seemed to have the support of the other two. Rose nodded in agreement and returned to her booth; Reg, muttering to himself, went to attend to a customer who'd put a coin into a machine and had nothing happen in return. Harry was left facing Nick who, arms folded and scowling, seemed determined on total non-cooperation.

'So you want treating as casual labour then . . . ?'

'That was the idea.'

'Then you might as well get yourself in there,' he said, indicating the change booth.

With little option, since he was still hoping to win the young man over, Harry allowed himself to be shut inside the small kiosk. There was a counter on which were neat stacks of coins, and a hole in the window through which he was to pass them to the punters. It was in their pound-notes and fivers that the real profit would accumulate; the coins he gave out would be eternally recycled through the machines.

A change booth wasn't the ideal spot from which to conduct an investigation. He could neither talk to anybody nor explore the premises; they couldn't have found a better way of frustrating him if they'd tried. More than once he caught sight of Nick and Reg chuckling together. No doubt they felt pleased at the way they'd not only put him in his place but in the one place where he was powerless.

It became a long day. There was a meal-break when he wandered out to buy some fish and chips and enjoy a few minutes of sunshine, then it was back to the piles of pennies. His only diversion was in watching the punters. There was a test-your-strength machine within his limited vision. He watched a young man approach, check that his girlfriend's attention was elsewhere, then have a go. Obviously it must have been a decent score – he called to his girlfriend for her to come and witness it. And was then disconcerted when she insisted on having a go herself and scored more than he'd done.

By mid-evening Harry's fingers were sore and dirty from handling the coins and he was beginning to feel distinctly rebellious. Gypsy Rose, on her way home, looked in at him through the glass and gave him a smile that had at least a hint of sympathy about it.

'How are you going on, love?'

'It's not a job I'd recommend,' said Harry, restraining himself.

'I'm sure it isn't, no,' she said. 'Good night then.'

He continued for another half-hour before deciding that enough was enough. Somebody else could take over; he was going to stretch his cramped limbs and take his turn at strolling about and watching the world go by, which was all Nick and Reg seemed to have been doing for most of the day.

'Right,' he said to Reg. 'I've done my stint. Somebody else's turn now.'

Reg, taken aback, looked round for Nick but found him nowhere to be seen.

'Well, I don't know,' he said weakly. 'I'm not sure about that.'

'I bloody well am,' said Harry, and left him standing there.

Coming to the front of the arcade, he was rewarded by a view of the sun just beginning to set over the sea, tinging the whole bay with a pinkish glow. The heat of the day had given way to an evening breeze that was refreshing after his hours of imprisonment. Across the promenade the pier was decked out in coloured lights. It was a sight that went some little way towards reminding him of the carefree holiday mood he'd been in earlier.

He returned to the arcade where Reg had taken over in the change booth.

'I'm going to make a cup of tea,' said Harry. 'Do you want one?'

Reg gave a grunt that might have meant anything.

'Sugar?'

Another grunt.

Harry let himself into the office at the rear of the arcade and put the kettle on. It was as much store-room as office so that, beside the desk and the large, ornate safe, there were buckets and brooms, money-bags, counting-machines, electric light-bulbs and drums of cleaning-fluid. There was also another door, one that seemed to offer admission to whatever remained of the original Winter Gardens ballroom.

Harry tried it and found it locked. He looked around for a key and found an embarrassment of choice, dozens of them strung together on chains and hanging from hooks on the wall. They'd be for the machines, of course, each one numbered. Then, at the end of the row, he came to a more ordinary-looking bunch. The second one he tried opened the door and he stepped through into the echoing, dusty vault of the abandoned ballroom.

Not that there was space for much more than a slow waltz. The plasterboard shell of the arcade took up most of what had been the dance-floor. A few steps from where Harry had entered and you reached the stage.

Harry hoisted himself on to it, then found his hands covered by a thick dust. He stepped cautiously to the side of the stage and peered into the areas beyond. There wasn't much to be seen, or enough light to see it by, just a general impression of passages going away. Running round three sides of the ballroom hung a balcony, its once decorative plasterwork cracked and dilapidated. The high roof above had just a few areas of glass remaining; the rest was boarded over.

'Found what you were looking for?'

It was a sudden challenge that made Harry's heart skip. He spun round. Someone had come through the doorway after him, a tall, slim figure silhouetted against the light inside the office. It was Nick. Nick who'd come back and followed him.

'Not yet,' said Harry curtly.

'I'm surprised. You being a detective and all that.'

Harry ignored the sarcasm. 'What's behind here?'

'Nothing you need concern yourself about.'

'Well, why don't you let me be the judge of that, eh?'

'There's not supposed to be anybody back here.'

'Who says?'

'Mr Underhill says. This was where we had somebody messing with the electrics the other day.'

'Give me a torch.'

'No,' said Nick stubbornly.

Harry crossed the stage, felt with his foot for its edge, then dropped to the floor.

'Listen, son,' he said, 'I can do without all this aggro.'

'And we can do without being spied on.'

'You're not being spied on. At least not by me.'

'Doesn't look like it, does it. What're you doing back here then if it's not spying?'

Harry hesitated, tempted to make an issue of it and teach the young man some manners. He saw Nick stiffen and his hands clench as he, too, recognised the dangerous moment for what it was. Then he thought what the hell, and decided to let it go.

A year ago he wouldn't have done. Up to meeting Jill he wouldn't have done. It was she who'd made him less sensitive about his honour and less quick to resort to his fists.

'Have it your own way,' he said with a smile. He waited till Nick stepped out of his path, said, 'Thank you,' and went through the doorway back into the office. He pulled off the nylon jacket they'd given him to wear and tossed it on to the desk.

'I'm off. I'm sure you can manage without me.'

'There's another hour yet,' objected Nick.

Harry smiled. 'Don't push your luck, son. And try and get a good night's kip. 'Cause I think it'd be in everybody's interest if you was to be in a better mood tomorrow. Good night.'

There was no reply. He went out through the arcade and, with not much idea where he was heading, turned into the first pub he saw. It was crowded and noisy and it took him a while to get served. There was a piano in the other bar and an air of jollity everywhere that he found difficult to share. Alone amid the crowd, he wasn't on holiday.

So where did he go from here? Bed-and-breakfast at Floribunda, then back to the arcade again tomorrow? It wasn't an attractive prospect but he was, after all, being paid — and paid well — for the job. He had to battle on a bit longer before ringing Derek Underhill and throwing in the towel.

Perhaps Rose might prove more amenable if he could speak to her alone. He'd sensed she'd entered reluctantly into the conspiracy against him. It was Nick who was ring-leader, with Reg taking his cue from the younger man.

He finished his pint and wandered out, looking for the road on which he was lodging. It seemed further away than it had that morning but still he found it all right and went into the lighted hallway.

There were voices to his right and he looked in to what was obviously the lounge and where half-a-dozen people were talking. He was about to start up the stairs when a voice said, 'Ah, Mr Sommers, isn't it?' and he saw that Mrs Melling was one of those in the lounge. 'Would you like some tea or coffee, Mr Sommers?'

'No, thanks,' he said, knowing he'd find the bonhomie of his fellow-guests even harder to take than the hostility of Nick and his pals. Then he remembered something he did want. 'Is there a phone I could use?'

'Yes. Right there in the hallway.'

He found it and lined up some ten-pence pieces, then had difficulty remembering the number, what with it being such a new one, but eventually he got through and there was Jill on the other end.

'You solved everything yet?' she asked.

'No.' And he gave her a run-down on the day's calamities, making them sound more amusing than they had been and omitting to mention that it'd been his own name the undertakers had been given.

'It sounds like a madhouse down there.'

'It feels like one.'

'You haven't been on the beach then.'

'Not a lot, no. And what have you been up to?'

'Painting.'

'Anybody call?'

'No. Good thing too. Anything comes in here at the moment gets covered in emulsion.'

They chatted some more about the day then, oddly, there

wasn't anything left to say. He heard her stifle a yawn.

'You sound tired. Go to bed and I'll ring you tomorrow.'

'I think I'd better. Oh, and I might be out for some of the day.'

'Don't worry, I'll keep trying.'

'Bye then. And I love you.'

'I love you,' he said, wondering whether they could hear him in the lounge.

He sat up in his attic bedroom and read some more of *Brighton Rock*. The gang-leader, and instigator of Hale's murder, was a young man named Pinkie. A very young man: no more than seventeen. He seemed an unlikely character to Harry who'd known a fair cross-section of East End villains but never one so puritanical and conscience-stricken. And seventeen . . . ? It seemed young to be getting up to extortion and murder though admittedly they left school earlier in those days. He let the book drop to the floor and fell asleep.

The four youths who wandered into the Winter Gardens arcade the following morning were all a year or two older than Pinkie's seventeen. They were wearing big boots, studded leather jackets and crash-helmets. No concessions to the weather here: as far as they were concerned it might have been mid-winter. One of them began to play a pin-ball machine while the other three gathered round, resting their elbows on it. All four were looking about them as if assessing the situation.

Alerted by this, Reg called to Nick from the change booth: 'What d'you think that little lot might be up to?'

Nick glanced at them. 'Don't know. Can't say I'm all that interested.'

'They look like trouble to me.'

'Everything looks like trouble to you, Reg. The Salvation Army looks like trouble to you. You're getting old, that's what it is.'

'Oh, am I? Well, we'll see, shall we? 'Appen I'm not as old or as stupid as you seem to think.'

The truth of which was on the point of being demonstrated when Harry arrived back at the arcade, having been on a small tour of the immediate neighbourhood.

He'd had a fitful night's sleep and a hearty breakfast, then turned up at the arcade to find that Nick and Reg were ignoring his existence and Gypsy Rose was occupied with a queue of customers wanting to know their futures. All in all there wasn't much point in his hanging around and so he'd taken himself along the promenade to visit some of the rival establishments — 'Blue Lagoon', 'Golden Horseshoe', 'Coral Island' — to see if they, too, had been on the receiving end of any funny business.

No, they hadn't, was the general response. Together with, And what do you want to know for? Which Harry answered by saying he was a newspaper reporter researching an article. He drew a blank in six or seven such places and got back to the Winter Gardens just in time to see four yobboes in black leather rocking a pin-table till it was in danger of going over and Nick shouting 'Hey . . . !' and moving in to stop them.

For a moment they seemed not to notice him — just went on rocking the table. Then they turned as one and went for him. Alarmed, Nick lashed out in wild defence but collected a kick or two before managing to dodge behind a bank of slot-machines, though by doing so he trapped himself, gaining a respite that could only be temporary.

Harry had watched in stunned disbelief. Now he came to life, bounding down the length of the arcade past Reg who had locked himself inside his change booth. He reached the first of the motorcyclists as they were moving in on Nick. He swung him round with one hand and threw a punch to the midriff with the other. Then, as the youth doubled over with a grunt of pain and surprise, Harry grabbed hold of him and used his helmeted head as a battering-ram to put paid to motorcyclist number two, who gave a yell of pain and fell to the floor holding his groin.

With the odds shortened to two against two, the defenders had now become the aggressors and the surviving yobboes were looking for a way out. Nick, wanting revenge for the working-over they'd promised him before Harry had arrived, set about one of them, bouncing him against the wall till his motorcycle visor became flecked with blood. The last, seeking to evade Harry and make his escape, ran into a video-machine and hobbled out, clutching his shoulder.

The others were now intent only on escape. Nick was happy to help them along with kicks and blows. It was only when it was too late and they'd more or less scarpered that Harry thought to call out, 'No. Grab one of 'em!' But they were beyond grabbing, disappearing into the crowds on the promenade. Back in the arcade the customers were asking one another what on earth had happened and what had they seen, frightened but also a little proud at having been close witnesses to violence.

'You all right?' asked Harry of Nick.

'Yes, fine,' he said, though there was a cut on his cheek and he was touching his side gingerly.

'I said they was bother, didn't I?' said Reg, approaching.

'That's about all you did,' said Nick. 'Not a lot of help, were you?'

'Somebody has to stop with the money.'

Nick turned to Harry. 'Hey, listen. Thanks. You did me a big favour then.'

Harry shrugged. 'Not all that big. I'm supposed to be employed here as well, don't forget.'

'It still didn't mean you had to get involved in that. 'Specially after the way I've been pissing you about.' He held out his hand. 'I'm very grateful.'

Harry took the offered hand and said, 'Well, I'd be just as grateful if we could all start working on the same side, all right?'

Nick managed a smile. 'Definitely. It was Reg here that was against you, wasn't that right, Reg?'

'You what?'

'Never mind. Just make us a cup of tea, eh.'

'Listen to him,' said Reg to Harry. 'You'd think he was the gaffer round here.' And then went to make the tea.

Gypsy Rose arrived, wanting to know what the commotion had been about. She was given a potted version and, taking her lead from Nick's new attitude, told Harry he was a hero. Indeed she seemed as relieved as he was that the period of hostilities was over. It amused Harry to observe how the two-minute fracas had elevated him from spy to saviour. Reg brought him a cup of tea and was sent back to bring another one for Rose.

'So tell me,' she said, 'were these hooligans anything to do with the other trouble we've been having or what?'

'Might have been,' said Harry. 'Don't suppose we'll ever know.'

'It seemed planned to me,' said Nick. 'I mean, all right, you do sometimes get people messing with the machines and then they don't like it when you tell 'em to stop. But they still don't react like these lads did. Not all together like that.'

'So where's it going to end?' asked Rose.

'Perhaps it already has,' said Harry, trying to sound more optimistic than he felt. 'Perhaps the reception we gave 'em will discourage 'em from trying anything else.'

'Let's hope so,' said Rose. 'Only I have a feeling it's going to get worse before it gets better. And for once I'll be very happy to be proved wrong.'

Nick winked at Harry, which meant don't take any notice of Rose's predictions and which also meant he and Harry were now allies, comrades-in-arms. As further measure of which he insisted that Harry shouldn't concern himself with the routine demands of the arcade but should be free to get on with his private investigating. Harry said thanks, finished his tea and wandered out again into the sunshine. With little else to go on, he might as well complete his tour of the resort's other arcades.

By mid-afternoon he'd walked the length of the promenade in each direction and discovered there were more slot-machine arcades in St Stephen's Bay than he'd thought possible. Derek

Underhill's establishment was distinctive in being housed in the largest and oldest building around; otherwise they were all much of a type: kiddies' rides at the front, rows of one-arm bandits inside, then the pool-tables and the pin-ball machines and the shooting-ranges at the back. Add to that somebody dishing out change and an earful of pop music and there didn't seem much to distinguish one from another. So why should the Winter Gardens have been singled out for such special and unwelcome attention?

'Any luck?' asked Nick when he returned.

He shook his head. 'If anybody is having any bother then they're not telling.'

Nor did he think they had anything to tell. He'd been met everywhere by puzzled denials. One or two had even laughed and told him he'd been watching too many gangster films.

'All right if I have a poke around in the back?' he asked Nick.

'Course it is. Anything you like.'

Daylight revealed the extent of the old ballroom's decline. There were patches of damp coming down the walls and broken glass and chunks of plaster piled into corners. The stage had a hole six foot wide in its centre. Miraculously, he must have stepped around it last night without ever seeing it.

Moving cautiously, he began to explore back-stage, surmounting an obstacle-course of rusting flood-lights and music-stands. There was a tiny scampering of mice somewhere ahead. A corridor brought him to what once must have been the dressing-rooms with their wash-basins and cracked mirrors still in place. One still had some post-cards drawing-pinned to the wall. A faded message read: 'Best wishes for a successful season. Love and kisses, Amanda.' All evidence of good times now long passed, but none to suggest this might be where their current troubles had their origins.

He returned to the office and re-locked the door. After the silence of the deserted ballroom he was struck by the clatter of money from within the arcade. Surely that was what this was all about: that continuous stream of coins that made your hands grubby and your life so much easier.

'You fancy a pint?' Nick asked. It was the evening and things had gone quiet.

'What a wonderful idea,' said Harry.

Reg protested about being left but Nick promised they'd be back in time for him to knock off early. Then he led Harry to a quiet little pub, tucked away in the streets off the promenade where the holiday-makers couldn't find it.

'How did you get into this job then?' asked Harry as they settled in a corner with their drinks.

'I was sort of bumming around and . . . well, I don't know really. I did a season on the deck-chairs, then when that was finished I had to look for something else and they were wanting somebody in the arcade so there I was.'

'And how long ago was that?'

'Oh . . . going on three years now.'

'You're from round here?'

'No. I come from Norwich.'

'Yes? And so what's this place got that Norwich hasn't?'

'Well, for one thing it's got jobs. And, for another, it's got birds. Can't want better than that, can you?'

Put like that, it sounded like a young man's paradise.

'You like the job then?'

'It's OK. Diabolical hours, but most of it's just standing around and the pay's good.'

'You don't get many customers like the four you got today?'

He shook his head. 'I'd be wanting a helluva sight more money if we did.'

'And so what's your interpretation of all that's been happening then?'

Nick shrugged. 'Looks like somebody's got it in for us.'

'Who?'

Another shrug: he didn't know.

'No ideas?' prompted Harry.

'None.'

'Has anybody ever been round asking for protection?'

'Not that I've been aware of. Why, is that what you think it's about?'

'Could be. Wouldn't be the first time somebody'd found himself with a load of problems, then some kind gent comes along and offers to take 'em all away in exchange for a small retainer.'

'Might be that then.'

'Might be. 'Cept I still can't see why they're picking on you and nobody else.' Then he added, surprising himself by the thought: 'Unless it's the building they're after.'

'What would they want that for?'

'No idea. I only just thought of it.'

'It's falling to pieces.'

'I know. But perhaps there's something in it . . . or under it or . . . well, I don't know, do I?'

'Buried treasure?' said Nick.

Harry looked and saw he was smiling, taking the mickey.

'Exactly. You ever had any one-legged customers with parrots on their shoulders?'

'Not recently.'

'Well, keep your eyes open. Another pint?'

Nick said yes and so Harry went to the bar where there was a collecting-tin for lifeboats and some old, brass telescopes displayed on the wall behind.

He was glad of the company of the young man whose hide he'd saved that morning, respecting him for the bold opposition he'd shown when Harry had first arrived and for the generous apology when he'd found himself in Harry's debt. There was a devil-may-care attitude about him that must work wonders with the ladies; nevertheless Harry trusted him and believed him when he claimed to know nothing of what was going on. Besides, he'd been himself the main object of this morning's attack; the cuts and grazes he bore were evidence enough of his innocence.

'What about Derek Underhill?' asked Harry, taking back the drinks.

'What about him?'

'What's he like as a boss?'

Nick made a gesture of indifference. 'All right.'

'Has he any enemies?'

'Hasn't everybody?'

'Anybody in particular though?'

This time Nick thought seriously about it, then said 'No.'

'How long has he had the arcade?'

'Oh . . . years. As long as there's been an arcade there.'

'And what about before that?'

'His family owned the Winter Gardens when it was a dancehall. He sort of inherited it.'

'So he won't be short of a bob or two.'

'Shouldn't be. 'Specially with the accounting system he's got. There's a lot of ready cash goes out of there the taxman doesn't know about.'

'I'll bet,' said Harry. 'But I doubt it's the taxman sending in yobboes to smash up the place. They have different ways of working.'

There was a pause as they both took a drink.

'How did you find out about me?' asked Harry.

'What, 'bout you being a private eye and all that?'

'Yes.'

Nick frowned, unable to remember, then said finally, 'I think it was Reg. He said you was one.'

'And how did he know?'

'He'd been talking to somebody. I don't know who — somebody that works for Charlie Monroe on the fair.'

It made sense. What was more natural than Charlie Monroe gossiping about how he'd run Derek Underhill to London in search of a private detective? It'd be worth a laugh over a drink and never mind that word might get passed on and Harry's anonymity jeopardised.

'You know Charlie Monroe?'

Harry sensed a new watchfulness come over the young man. He hadn't minded speculating about his boss, Derek Underhill, but now here was a more dangerous subject, one demanding greater caution.

'I've met him.'

'Tell me about him.'

'Why?'

'I just want to know, that's all.'

There was a moment when Harry thought he'd refuse, then he gave a small smile and said, 'He runs the fair and a few other things beside. Got stacks of money. Drives a Merc. Doesn't like it if people don't do what he says.'

'How d'you mean?' asked Harry, though knowing well enough. After all, he'd worked for the man in the past and witnessed the speed with which his genial good humour could slip into a sullen malevolence at an imagined or real slight. Still, it was worth getting another opinion.

'Oh, just that he fancies himself as the big man round here. Anybody wants to set up in the entertainments field they'd be wise to have a word with him.'

'You mean he's running some sort of racket? He'd want a share of the action?'

'Oh, I'm not saying that, no. He has more money than he knows what to do with anyway. No, he just likes throwing his weight about, that's all.'

'Where's he live?'

'Just out of town. A bloody great house with a paddock and a swimming-pool and everything. And then he has a flat in London. And I think one in Deauville as well. He likes playing the casinos in France.'

'You seem to know a lot about him.'

Nick met his gaze. 'It's all most people have got to talk about round here. Especially in winter.'

'You don't think he might have anything to do with the aggro you've been experiencing?'

Nick grimaced. 'I don't see why he'd bother.'

Harry had to agree. People with Charlie Monroe's property and Charlie Monroe's income and, more particularly, with Charlie Monroe's view of himself as the Mr Fix-it of St Stephen's Bay didn't stoop to lowly protection set-ups and risk blowing the lot. An up-and-coming, young Charlie Monroe maybe; but not a man who had it made to the extent of a Merc and playing chemin-de-fer in Deauville.

But Nick had something more to say.

'I'll tell you something he did once.'

'What?'

He leaned closer and spoke confidentially. 'There was once this dispute about who was running the donkeys on the south shore. Somebody was trying to muscle in on a friend of Charlie's. So this friend asked Charlie if he'd do something about it. And Charlie went to this other guy and told him to lay off. Only he didn't take any notice. So next thing that happens — he woke up one morning and went to his bathroom and you know what he found in his bath . . . ?'

'What?'

'The head of one of his donkeys.'

Harry looked at him, waiting for the give-away smile; but no, he wasn't joking.

'The Godfather touch,' said Harry.

'You've seen the film? Where he puts the race-horse's head in the bed?'

'Yes. And so that's how Charlie sees himself, is it? Godfather of St Stephen's Bay.'

'Something like that.'

'So long as it makes him happy,' said Harry, thinking of the time Charlie Monroe had held greater ambitions and made his abortive attempt at promotion to the premier league of the metropolis. It was probably better for everybody that he'd now settled for being a big fish in a small, sea-water pond.

They decided it was time to relieve Reg and so set off back to the arcade. It was a warm, clear evening, promising that the hot weather would continue for a while yet. They came on to the promenade. The sun had gone down and the sea was an inky black beyond the coloured lights of the pier.

'You're not joking, are you?' asked Harry as they arrived at the arcade.

'What about?'

'The donkey's head.'

'No, I'm not joking. It's well-known. You ask anybody.'

'He made him an offer he couldn't refuse,' recited Harry, remembering the film.

Reg was glad to see them back and hurried off to the Grand where he'd now manage an extra hour's drinking. Harry stood looking out to the horizon, thinking how little he understood about the nature of the universe and even less about the nature of this particular case.

5

A fat man, with rolling stomach piled upon rolling stomach, paddled at the sea's edge, oblivious to the crab gripping his big toe. Behind him, a midget boy guzzled an ice-cream. 'Has anybody seen my little Willie?' demanded the fat man of an outraged and equally fat lady.

The card below that depicted a small, seedy-looking man who wore his hair parted down the middle. To one side of him was a sign — 'Bird Sanctuary'; to the other was his elephantine wife. 'My word,' he said to her as he focused his binoculars on a distant, topless sunbather, 'they're the finest pair of tits I've seen this year.'

They were rude and jolly in primary colours, as much a part of the traditional holiday scene as were the sands and the pier and the donkeys. There was a rackful of them outside the newsagent's that was next door to the Winter Gardens. Harry stood leafing through, amused and pleased to find they'd survived with their innocence intact.

Another card showed a nudist camp — a sign, slightly askew, announced it as such. An amazingly-proportioned female was wearing a guitar and asking a wide-eyed male (whose embarrassment was saved by a protruding shrubbery), 'Sorry to trouble you, but would you mind having a look at my G-string?'

Harry stepped away from the rack, reminding himself he was being paid to watch the arcade, not to chortle over dirty postcards. Then he noticed he'd stepped into the line of someone's camera. 'Sorry,' he said, instinctively ducking out of the way and then turning to see who was being photographed.

But there was no-one there to be photographed. No-one behind him at all. It took a second or two before he understood what was happening and by then the photographer had disappeared.

The camera had been pointing at him. The photographer had been waiting there for him to turn away from the rack of postcards before snapping him. There couldn't have been any other subject for his picture.

Stunned by the realisation, Harry tried to make sense of it. Who in their right mind would want a picture of him standing outside a newsagent's on the promenade of St Stephen's Bay? And, whoever it was, why should they then have legged it the moment the picture was taken? It certainly wasn't your common-or-garden seaside photographer who would have been keener to sell than to escape. So who on earth was it?

Not knowing and unable to do anything about finding out, Harry went back into the arcade, where it was business as usual with Nick eyeing the girls, Reg guarding the change and Gypsy Rose retailing various versions of the future.

'You all right?' asked Nick, observing him.

'Yes.'

'Only you look as if you've seen a ghost.'

'No, I'm all right,' said Harry, deciding to keep the photographer incident to himself for the time being. 'I thought I might go and have a word with Charlie Monroe. D'you know where I might find him?'

Nick hesitated. 'Charlie Monroe . . . ?'

'Yes.'

'What d'you want to talk to him for?'

'Nothing specific. Only if, as you say, he likes to think he knows everything that's going on — well, maybe he'll have an idea about what went on here yesterday.'

'I doubt it.'

'So do I. But I'd like to have a word with him all the same.'

Nick still hesitated, clearly not keen. Frightened by Charlie Monroe's reputation, thought Harry.

'Look, don't worry,' he said reassuringly. 'I know Charlie of old. I used to work for him.'

'You never said,' said Nick, some of the old suspicion coming back into his manner.

'You never asked. Now come on. All I want you to tell me is where I'm likely to find him at this time of the day.'

Nick shrugged. 'Fairground I suppose. He has an office on the far side. After you pass the Haunted House but before you get to the Ghost Train.'

The fairground at St Stephen's Bay wasn't Disneyland but it did have the usual range of rides and side-shows. The Big Wheel was reasonably big and the Big Dipper did a fair amount of dipping. There were also Dodgems and Carousels, a Hall of Mirrors, various shooting-galleries and coconut shies, a Water Chute, a device that whirled you round upside down and another that whirled you round the right way up. There was a Helter-Skelter, a Tunnel of Love, a Caterpillar, a Snake and an Octopus, all of which were rides and not animals.

Harry allowed himself a wander round before seeking out Charlie Monroe. Most of the rides were at least thirty pence a go; some were fifty; and all had queues waiting. You could see where the money for the Twickenham business had come from. You could also see why Charlie Monroe fancied himself as a man of influence around town. The fairground was probably as close as you could get to the resort's beating heart; whoever owned it had his finger on the pulse.

Harry located the Haunted House and saw a building next to it that might well have been an office — at least it didn't have coloured lights and music coming from it. He headed towards it, then found he'd timed things perfectly: there was Charlie emerging from the office door even as Harry reached it.

'Harry boy! Well, this is a surprise.'

'It shouldn't be. You got me the job, remember?'

Charlie snapped his fingers. 'Derek Underhill. You're sorting out his little problems for him.'

'Trying to.'

He sensed Charlie was in a hurry to be off. Certainly he wasn't making any move to escort Harry back into the office but was edging further away from it even as he spoke.

'And how long are you down here for?'

'Couple of weeks. Depends on how things go.'

'Well then we must have a drink. Look, give me a bell, eh. Only I'm a bit pushed at the moment, you know how it is.'

'Yes, OK,' said Harry. But he stuck with him as they walked through the crowds, thinking he might get more out of Charlie off guard and in a hurry than he ever would when he wasn't. 'Only the thing is, see — I'd appreciate some advice.'

'What kind of advice?'

'About this business of Derek Underhill's. I feel I'm a bit up against it at the moment.'

They came past a shooting-gallery. The young girl running it gave Charlie a small smile of recognition as they passed. Next was a children's roundabout. This was presided over by a large, unshaven man with a beer gut who bawled, 'All right, Mr Monroe?'

Charlie saluted him, then turned back to Harry. 'How d'you mean — up against it?'

'With not knowing the place. Not knowing the people and who might be making trouble for who. I mean I'm a long way off my own manor, if you see what I mean.'

'Well, yes, but it's like toy town is this. Compared with what you've been accustomed to.'

'It's still no good if I don't know the people,' persisted Harry. 'That's why I wondered — have you any idea who might have it in for Derek Underhill?'

'Not a clue. I mean, be fair, Harry boy — if I knew who it was then I could have helped him sort it. What with Derek being a long-standing mate. I wouldn't have had to recommend you then, would I?'

'You don't know if he has any enemies?'

'None. He's well-liked is Derek. Pillar of the community. No, I think you're barking up the wrong tree there, I do.'

He had to raise his voice against the raucous laughter issuing from the Laughing Policeman — a dummy in a glass-case that guffawed relentlessly, attracting a small crowd who stood in front of it and smiled back.

Outside the fairground entrance, a silver Mercedes was parked on double-yellow lines.

'All right then,' said Harry. 'Let me try you with another idea.'

'And what's that?'

'You don't think anybody might be trying to muscle in? Offer protection?'

Charlie grinned. 'You obviously are a long way off your manor, Harry boy. This isn't your East End now. This isn't even your West End. This is the bloody seaside where we're all straight and above-board.'

One of the Mercedes' tinted windows slid open and Harry saw there was someone already inside and waiting. It was a young woman — much younger than Charlie, or than Harry himself come to that. She had piled blonde hair and a pouting, spoiled expression, which was a pity since, with a smile on her face, she might just have been the best-looking woman Harry had seen for quite some time. She said nothing; just glanced at Harry, then looked meaningfully at Charlie.

'Yes, all right, doll,' said Charlie. 'I'm here. And in a minute we'll be off. Don't worry.'

The tinted window slid silently shut.

'We've got to have lunch with some poncy geezers from the golf club,' explained Charlie. 'Personally I'd rather not bother, but you know what women are like when it gives 'em a chance to show off their sun-tans.'

'Have a nice time,' said Harry.

'Oh, I will. Though she'd rather I didn't 'cause she's frightened I'll start telling dirty stories if I get pissed.' He laughed. 'Which of course I probably will. You know sometimes I think they only invite me 'cause I have more money than the rest of 'em put together.' He reached for the handle of the car door, then paused and added: 'By the way, that is the missus in there. Just in case you were wondering.'

'I never wonder about things like that,' said Harry. 'Anyway, didn't I meet her? That time you brought her up to see the club?'

Charlie looked quickly to see the tinted window was still closed and stepped back towards Harry before saying, 'No, that was the old model was that. I ditched her a couple of years back and got a new one.'

'You've got good taste,' said Harry, glad Jill couldn't hear him. She'd explained to him what sexism meant and made him self-conscious about jokes that put down women.

'Dead right I have,' grinned Charlie, who had no such inhibitions. 'I was born with it. Now don't forget what I said. Give us a bell and we'll have a few jars together.'

Harry nodded. Charlie opened the door on the driver's side of the Mercedes and climbed in, leaving the faint, sweet scent of after-shave behind him.

He also left Harry thinking of Jill. The momentary self-consciousness when he'd chortled over Charlie's wife-swapping had made him now want to speak to her and remind her of her promise to come down and join him. It had been a vague arrangement and he had the uneasy feeling that if he didn't do something about it — and quickly — then as like as not it would remain unfulfilled till his two weeks were up and he returned to their flat in Islington.

He walked back to the arcade — where, thank God, nothing out-of-the-ordinary had been happening — and shut himself in the office. The first time he rang her there was no reply so he came out again and chatted to Nick and Reg until half-an-hour had passed and he then went back into the office and tried again. This time she was there at the other end of the line.

'How's it going?' she asked when she heard his voice.

'Not too good. I don't know whether I'm going to be able to find out very much. How's the painting?'

There was a pause, then she said simply, 'Sticky.'

He laughed, pleased to be talking to her again and remembering why he loved her: because she was smarter than he was and knew more than he'd ever know, yet needed his uncomplicated approach to life as a swimmer in a storm might cling to a life-raft.

'How're you sleeping?' he asked.

'Oh, not too bad. What about you?'

'Terrible. I'm missing you.'

'Oh well, I'm missing you as well,' she said quickly. 'Just that if there's one thing to be said for painting it does make you sleep at nights.'

'We said you'd come down and join me.'

'I know we did.'

'So when're you coming?'

'When do you want me?'

He felt she was fencing: waiting for him to make his move, then she could block it.

'Tomorrow,' he said boldly.

'All right then. I'll be down tomorrow.'

It was a response that surprised and even silenced him for a moment. Though it'd been agreed she should join him after two or three days — which meant tomorrow or thereabouts — he'd never fully believed she would. Perhaps it was her odd insistence that he should take the job in the first place that had left him with the impression she wanted them to be apart for a while.

But that she should now be wanting to join him tomorrow — that was wonderful.

'Yes, sure. What time?'

'Well, I don't know. I'll have to find out about trains.'

'There's more or less one every hour. What were you thinking — tomorrow morning?'

'Oh no. And you wouldn't either if you could see the state of this place. No, definitely not morning. More like tomorrow evening if I can manage it.'

'And what time?'

'I don't know what time.'

He sensed she was becoming impatient.

'Well look, ring me here as soon as you decide on the train and then I can pick you up at the station.'

'Yes. But it won't be before seven or eight. Don't expect me before that.'

She sounded defeated . . . resigned. As if joining him were something beyond her control. He detected a warning in her tone: that she'd be there but he wasn't to expect too much.

'It'll be great to see you, whatever time,' he said, settling for her minimum terms. He'd already had ample experience of her moods, her unpredictable dives into depression, and could only hope the holiday atmosphere would work on her spirit in the way it had worked on his. Though he feared she was more complex: that, for her, donkeys and deck-chairs might be as much a turn-off as a tonic.

In the meantime he'd better get to work on Mrs Melling. Jill seemed to have taken it for granted she'd be moving in with him; and there was room certainly: the three-quarter bed and the attic room could take them both. It was just a matter of smoothing the way.

He went back to Floribunda and found Mrs Melling in the dining-room, shining up the silver toast-racks.

'I've just been on the phone to my wife,' he said. 'She's thinking of coming down to join me for a few days. Would it be OK if we called it a double booking and she moved in with me?'

'Your wife, you say?'

Clearly she didn't believe him. For which he couldn't altogether blame her: after all, Jill wasn't his wife and probably wouldn't thank him for saying she was.

'Yes.'

'I don't normally let that room as a double.'

Harry stood and waited.

'Well, all right then,' she said finally. 'You'd find it very difficult to get anywhere else just now.'

'I'm very grateful,' said Harry. 'We both are.' And he backed out of the dining-room.

Mrs Melling gave a sniff of disdain and attacked the toast-racks with renewed vigour.

The remainder of the day Harry spent on sentry duty at the arcade, giving himself an hour off to sit in the sun and read *Brighton Rock*, which turned into two hours when he fell asleep over it. Hurrying back to the arcade, he noticed a gang of motor-cyclists lazing on the promenade steps, but whether their raiders of yesterday were among them he couldn't say. Their black regalia that so marked them out from among the crowd made them difficult to identify one from another. He stared challengingly in their direction, thinking he might provoke a telling reaction but none of them so much as blinked an eyelid.

'You've caught the sun,' said Rose, when he got back to the arcade and found her in the office, brewing up.

'It's about all I have caught,' said Harry wryly.

'Ah now, don't be like that,' said Rose. 'Let me look at your hand.'

He held out his right hand and she peered into the palm.

'Oh well, this is good. You've got a very strong life-line — and a very strong love-line too — though it diverges at various points. You're never going to make a lot of money. But then what's money against good health?'

That night was one of the nights set aside for collecting the money in from the machines. It was a ritual performed twice a week during the holiday season and once a week out of it. Harry had been told of it by Nick and been happy to volunteer his assistance in the place of the absent Derek Underhill.

They closed the arcade half-an-hour earlier than usual. Once the steel shutters were in place and locked, they brought out the buckets and the counting-machines and the money-bags.

'All right,' said Nick, 'see if we can break the record, shall we?'

And they set to work with a will, opening each machine in turn, unloading the coins inside into the buckets, then emptying the buckets into the counting-machines, and then bagging the coins as they came spewing out of the other end. Harry found he was enjoying himself. He was glad of the exercise and amused by the nature of the operation. He'd seen deals done before with handfuls of fivers or fistfuls of tenners and once, in a club he'd been minding off Shaftesbury Avenue, with a tiny bagful of diamonds, but never had he seen coins weighed in by the bucketful.

After a while it became hard work and the pace began to flag. Reg, in particular, made no bones about having to rest.

'It's all right for you young 'uns,' he panted. 'Wait till you get to my age.'

'And what age is that?' called Nick.

'You mind your own bloody business.' Then, as Harry was passing him with a loaded bucket in each hand, he lowered his voice and said, 'Hey.'

Harry stopped. 'What?'

'I've got something to tell you.'

'What about?'

Reg looked to see Nick wasn't listening, then said, 'Not here. I'll tell you after.'

'All right.'

'We'll go for a drink.'

It was another hour before they began to see an end to their task. The place had become hotter as they'd worked. They'd discarded their shirts and opened what few windows they could but the air remained heavy, not just from their sweaty efforts, but from the smell and taste of the money itself.

Finally it was done. The bandits and the pin-balls and the rest of the machines were closed and relocked, the book-keeping was completed — 'In pencil,' as Nick pointed out, 'so Derek can change it later' — and the bagfuls of money were stuffed into the safe till it wouldn't take any more and the excess had to go in a filing-cabinet. They came out of the arcade, grateful for the cool night air on their faces.

'Well thanks, Harry,' said Nick. 'I'd have been there all night with just this useless old bugger to help me.'

Reg ignored the remark and spat into the gutter.

'My pleasure,' said Harry. 'It's the nearest I'll ever get to working in a bank.'

'Nearest any of us'll get,' laughed Nick. 'Anyhow I'm off. Got some business to attend to.'

'Oh, and what's her name tonight then?' leered Reg.

'I've told you before,' said Nick. 'I never ask their names. Saves complications later.'

And, with a knowing wink at Harry, he was away along the promenade.

'He'll go blind will that lad,' said Reg, shaking his head. 'Else get some disease.'

'You sound jealous,' joked Harry.

'Not really. I prefer a nice drink any time. Come on. I know where they'll still serve us.'

He led Harry to the Grand Hotel, which wasn't quite so salubrious as its name implied but which did have a residents' lounge where the bar was open and Reg was known.

'I'll have to buy the drinks,' he said to Harry. 'Though you can give me the money for 'em if you like.'

They settled in an alcove, which seemed to satisfy Reg, who looked around them cautiously before beginning to talk.

'It's something I thought you might like to know.'

Harry waited patiently.

'It's about the arcade.'

Harry nodded.

'Though of course I can't say for sure whether it's anything to do with the bother we've been having. I mean I'm not pointing the finger, I'm just telling you what I know and then it's up to you if you want to take it any further.'

'Fair enough.'

'Only, see, I've been there for quite a few years now and so Mr Underhill takes me into his confidence in a way he wouldn't do with the young lad.'

Harry doubted the truth of that but let it go. Just gave a nod that suggested he, too, was in Mr Underhill's confidence and so it was all right for them to talk.

'And I'll tell you something now that very few people know,' said Reg. 'That building is worth a million pounds.'

'What building? The arcade?'

'The whole lot. The old ballroom and everything.'

'And why is it worth a million pounds?'

'Well, when I say a million, I don't mean a million exactly. But a helluva lot of money. On account of the planning permission it has.'

'What planning permission?'

'Oh yes, I thought that'd come as a surprise.'

'It does,' said Harry. 'What was the planning permission for?'

It was like getting blood from a pebble, but he was encouraged by the feeling that, for all Reg's determination to play the suspense to the hilt, he might nevertheless actually know something of importance.

'The planning permission . . .' said Reg slowly, 'the planning permission . . . for converting it into a casino.'

'Casino . . . ?' echoed Harry in surprise.

'I thought that'd make you sit up and take notice,' said Reg, pleased with himself.

'You mean Derek Underhill has got planning permission to turn the Winter Gardens into a casino?'

'No.'

Harry sighed. 'So what do you mean?'

'It wasn't Mr Underhill that got the permission.'

'Who was it?'

'Charlie Monroe.'

Harry stared at him. Reg grinned and nodded, with the

triumphant air of a magician who's just produced a rather larger-than-average rabbit.

'Charlie Monroe it was that got it. You don't have to own the property you're getting the planning permission on, you see. Oh no. Not if you're thinking of buying it later.'

'So Charlie Monroe applied for planning permission to turn the Winter Gardens into a casino,' said Harry slowly.

'I knew you'd be interested.'

'But was it granted?'

'Yes. Course it was. That's what I'm telling you. He got the planning permission, no problem.'

'And he was intending to buy the place, was he?'

'I imagine he was. Must have been to have gone to all that trouble.'

'So what happened? Why didn't he?'

'Ah well,' said Reg, taking a sip of his beer 'that's where you've got me. I mean Mr Underhill takes me only so far into his confidence. So you'd better be asking him that.'

Perhaps I had, thought Harry. He couldn't yet see how the pieces fitted but at least he was beginning to have the feeling they might belong to the same jigsaw. Certainly the Winter Gardens seemed to be the one arcade in the resort singled out for trouble. It was also the only arcade housed in such vast premises. And now here was a snippet of information that would make those premises a very valuable piece of real estate indeed.

'And how long ago was this?'

"Bout three years.'

'And Derek Underhill told you about it?'

'Yes.'

'But he didn't tell Nick.'

'Nick wasn't there then. It was before Nick arrived.'

'And you're sure it was Charlie Monroe?'

'Definite. I know Charlie Monroe any day of the week. Everybody does. And then Rose showed me the notice in the newspaper that had his name attached to it. Asking if anybody had any objections and all that.'

'And nobody did?'

'Not as I know of. Can't have had, can they, since it was granted?'

True, thought Harry. That was logical enough, though the rest of it wasn't. If Charlie Monroe had gone to the trouble of applying for and being granted planning permission on the Winter Gardens then why hadn't he proceeded with it? He was certainly ambitious to expand his empire: his foray into London had proved that. And he had the cash and connections to mastermind the establishing of a casino in St Stephen's Bay.

Perhaps Derek Underhill had realised the value of his property and refused to sell. But then why hadn't he gone ahead himself with the casino development?

And why did Charlie Monroe keep insisting that Derek Underhill was a good mate of his? He'd hardly be doing so if there were a history of friction over the sale of the Winter Gardens between them.

And last, but not least, where did three tons of liquid cement, two misguided undertakers and four bothersome motorcyclists fit into all this?

He decided to ask Reg. 'So what's the connection with all the bother we've been having?'

But Reg had gone as far as he intended. 'No use asking me that. You're supposed to be the detective. You tell me.'

'I can't.'

'So what do they pay you for then?'

Harry gave a tired smile. He remembered what Clifford Humphries, his predecessor, had said more than once.

'They pay you for poking about and asking unpleasant questions that they want to know the answers to but daren't ask. And they also pay you because it keeps their consciences happy, lets 'em feel they're doing everything they can. The trouble comes when you do everything you can and come up with the wrong answers. Or, even worse, come up with right answers when you weren't meant to.'

6

Next evening, just as the boarding-houses of St Stephen's Bay were serving dinner, and as an abrupt and bizarre side-effect of the continuing tropical temperatures, the entire south coast was blanketed in a dense mist.

The weathermen talked about radiation, a sudden cooling at sunset that deposited millions of tiny droplets from the saturated air. Other people claimed they'd known it was too good to last and recalled 1963 when it had snowed on midsummer's day and the outdoor swimming-pool had iced over. Cars switched on their headlights and the illuminations along the promenade came on early but to little effect: where the sea had been was now only a milky opacity and the faint sound of breakers.

Harry was at the arcade, as bemused as anyone by the change, when he received the promised phone-call from Jill saying she was at Victoria and on her way. She rang off quickly — he sensed the train waiting in the background — so that he could judge nothing of her mood. But she was coming: that was the important thing.

It was Nick's night off but Harry had already explained to Reg about his meeting with Jill and it'd been arranged that Gypsy Rose would help out in his absence.

With time to spare, he took a leisurely stroll along the promenade towards the station. He was intrigued by the freak conditions. It was as if a giant cloud had broken its moorings and floated to earth, providing not the icy fog of winter but something warmer and denser, almost comforting.

Except that, inevitably, it meant Jill's train would be late. A sign on the station forecourt announced: 'Due to poor visibility all trains are subject to delay.'

Harry went to the station buffet and ordered a cup of coffee. He wished now he'd brought along his copy of *Brighton Rock* to pass the time. Without it, he could only sip his coffee and wonder about the Winter Gardens and the new, tantalising possibilities that Reg's late-night revelations had opened up.

His first task that morning had been to check their accuracy. He'd made his way to the town's Planning Department and, after one or two false starts – since he wasn't all that clear on what he was looking for – he'd found a helpful official who'd searched the Buildings' Register and come up with a manilla file marked '62/68 Marine Parade – Winter Gardens'. Inside was a wad of plans and letters and documents, some ageing and yellowed, others more recent.

'Here we are,' said the official, plucking out a few of the newer-looking ones. 'I think this is what you're looking for.'

'What, they're plans to turn the place into a casino, are they?' asked Harry, trusting the official's interpretation to whatever he might make of them.

'Well, let's see . . . Here's where application was made . . . and here's where it was granted. May fifteenth, nineteen eighty-three. Subject to building regulations of course. But nobody seems to have raised any objections. And he's also got Listed Building Consent.'

'What's that?'

'Well, with buildings of special interest or merit, it's something you have to have before you can change their use or appearance.'

'And this is all in the name of Mr Monroe?'

He looked again. 'Yes.'

'Even though he doesn't own it . . . ?'

'Oh, does he not? Well, let's see what else there is in here then . . . . Well yes, you see here's a letter from a Mr Underhill – who I presume does own it . . . .'

'He does, yes.'

'A letter from Mr Underhill stating he's no objection to Mr Monroe applying for planning permission on his property.'

So Derek Underhill had known about it all along and been happy to let Charlie go ahead. Or at least he'd written a letter stating that he was.

'And all this — the planning permission and everything — is it still valid?' asked Harry.

The official looked again at the date. 'Oh yes. Once granted, it's valid for five years, so this still has a couple of years to run.'

'Have you any idea why Mr Monroe never took things any further?'

The official smiled politely. 'No idea at all I'm afraid. Though it's something that happens all the time. People come to us with all manner of schemes that we never hear any more about.'

'Oh, I see.'

'Was there anything else you wanted to know?'

Well yes, thought Harry, a hell of a lot. But it wasn't going to be found inside a file at the Planning Department.

The next thing had been to ring Yvonne. It was time he called her anyway, to find how she was coping single-handed, and now he had a more specific reason besides.

'Coronet Private Detective Agency,' she answered in her prim, telephone voice. 'Can I help you?'

'What do you know about casinos?'

'Harry!' she exclaimed. 'How are you? How's everything going?'

'Oh, it could be worse. At least I'm getting a sort of holiday out of it. I'm just not sure what I'm going to be able to offer Derek Underhill in return.'

'You can offer him a full report of your investigations, and leave him to draw his own conclusions,' she said swiftly.

He caught an echo of the sentiment he'd often heard advanced by Clifford Humphries: 'We're being paid to look under stones and round corners and into other people's business. And if all we find is nothing, then nothing is all we report. We don't have to feel guilty about that.'

All of which was no doubt true but easier said than done: people laying out good money expected solutions, not apologies.

He gave her a quick run-down on all that'd happened since he'd arrived.

'Well, good God,' she said, 'you've already defended his premises against a gang of thugs. What more can he want?'

'He wants to know who's behind it.'

'Does there have to be somebody behind it?'

'Well, it's a bit of a coincidence otherwise. All this aggro happening at once. Oh yes, and why should somebody want to take a picture of me?'

That silenced her for a moment.

'Who was it?'

'I don't know. I didn't realise what he was up to till it was too late and he'd scarpered.'

'And what were you doing at the time?'

'Just standing there, minding my own business.'

No point in complicating matters by mentioning the dirty postcards.

'Well, perhaps they were photographing the arcade and you just happened to get in the way.'

'Perhaps they were,' he said, though he couldn't believe it, hard as he tried: the camera had been aimed at him and had caught him before he could move away.

'Anyway,' she said, 'why were you asking about casinos?'

He told her about his tip-off from Reg and his researches at the Planning Department.

'Now if I remember rightly,' he said, thinking of the titbits he'd overheard when he was bouncer in one or another of London's gambling dens, 'there's a bit more to setting up a casino than just getting the OK from your local authority. Doesn't the Gaming Board come into it somewhere?'

'I suppose they must do. Wouldn't be called the Gaming Board otherwise, would they?'

'Do you think you can find out?'

'Well, I can try.' Then she added uneasily, 'Do be careful, won't you? I don't like the sound of all this. I thought the job was to do with slot-machine arcades, not casinos.'

'Don't worry,' said Harry. 'This is the seaside, not the West End. Any villains here have come for a holiday.'

To change the subject, he asked how she was managing the agency without him. This time it was her turn to be reassuring: she was up-to-date on the process-serving and surveillance work and was enjoying the opportunity to get out and about. There'd been just a couple of would-be clients who'd gone elsewhere on finding a woman holding the fort on her own. Otherwise, it was business as usual. She promised to get on to the Gaming Board as soon as she could and rang off.

'The seven-fifteen from Victoria, due at eight-twenty, is now running approximately thirty minutes late,' announced the tannoy.

Harry drained his coffee and went for a walk outside. The mist was persisting, obscuring the platforms beyond the ticket-barrier.

Of course, there was always the direct approach, he thought. He could knock on the door of Charlie Monroe's office and ask him outright about the planning application he'd made three years ago and why he'd never proceeded with it. For that matter he could also ask Derek Underhill about his role: was he to have gone into partnership with Monroe, or sold out to him, or what? But he was reluctant to approach either without first being sure of his facts and would therefore wait at least till Yvonne had reported back.

Strange, too, that Derek Underhill had made no mention of the casino plans when he'd rambled on to Harry about the hardships of running a slot-machine arcade, especially one occupying such extravagant premises. Nor had Charlie Monroe, though Harry's conversation with him had been cut short by his wife's impatience at being late for her lunch.

Could it be that some third party had become aware of the building's potential and had set to work to drive out Derek Underhill, first softening him up by causing havoc in the arcade, then stepping in later with an offer that Derek would be too demoralised to refuse. It would be an unorthodox and risky way of doing business.

Then, as quickly and unexpectedly as it had descended, the white mist evaporated away, revealing the remains of a pink sunset and Jill's train arriving on platform four.

He spotted her before she him and thought how much paler than her fellow-passengers she looked, probably the result of her days spent emulsioning the kitchen. It thrilled him as it always did to know she was his, this classy bird who knew how to dress and read *The Guardian* and was thus quite unlike any other woman he'd ever got within embracing distance of.

She saw him at last and gave a little wave. There was a final delay at the bottle-neck of the ticket-barrier, then she was through and in his arms.

'Bloody train,' she said. 'I'd have been quicker walking.'

'At least you're here. That's the main thing,' he said. Then felt, as he so often did with her, that he was talking in clichés.

He took her suitcase and they found a taxi. On the way to Floribunda, he explained about the problems of finding accommodation in the middle of the season but found her unconcerned and distracted. All she said when she saw the house with its printed notices and brass gong was, 'It's like something out of a Whitehall farce.'

Mrs Melling appeared, wearing a floral apron.

'Good evening, Mrs Sommers,' she said. 'I hope you had a pleasant journey.'

Jill gave Harry a baleful glance. Ah yes, he thought. I should have mentioned we're supposed to be married. She's not going to like that.

'Yes, thank you.'

'Well, I hope you enjoy your stay. Do let me know if there's anything you need,' said Mrs Melling stiffly.

'Mrs Sommers . . . ?' hissed Jill as they started the climb together. 'And so are we supposed to be on our honeymoon or what?'

'We can pretend to be if you like.'

'I'd like not to pretend at all,' she said.

They took the third and fourth flights without speaking and at last were in the room. Jill sat on the bed and looked round.

'There's a view of the sea,' said Harry, striving to be cheerful. 'But only if you lean out of the window and look between the chimney-pots.'

She said nothing.

'What's the matter?'

'I'm afraid I've brought some bad news.'

Harry stared. She's leaving me, he thought. It had to be. She'd come all that way to tell him she didn't want to see him again. Didn't want to live with him. Would finish emulsioning the kitchen, then move out. Yet her suitcase was full, suggesting she was staying for some days. Perhaps not then. What other kind of bad news was there?

'What?' he asked, setting himself as though for a blow.

'Greg's turned up again.'

'Greg . . . ?'

She nodded. 'Turned up at the flat the day after we moved in. God knows how he managed to track me down but there he was, large as life.'

Greg was her ex-husband; in fact, technically still her husband till the divorce, which he'd bitterly opposed throughout, had run its course. It had crossed Harry's mind more than once that a powerful reason for her moving into the Islington flat with him had been to escape Greg's persistent attentions.

Now it came as a relief to learn the bad news she'd brought him was no more than this. Annoying, and distressing for her, but surely something with which they could cope.

'I hope you told him what he can do with himself.'

'I've been trying to, yes. I've been trying for the past week.'

'You mean he's been pestering you?' said Harry, becoming concerned. 'He's been round more than once?'

'Yes. To be honest, it was why I wanted you to take this job. I thought it best if you were out of the way while I dealt with him.'

'Why?' he asked, resentful that she should have plotted to exclude him from a matter that might well have begun as hers alone but which couldn't remain so.

'I just thought it would be better. I knew you'd be furious if I told you.'

There'd already been an incident where Harry had encountered Greg hanging around outside her flat and, mistaking his identity, given him a bloody nose for his pains. It was a mistake that had all but ended his relationship with Jill once and for all.

'Somebody ought to teach him a lesson,' he muttered.

'It's not as simple as that.'

He made a great effort and said nothing, still wanting to challenge her on why he'd had to be evacuated to St Stephen's Bay so that the marital death throes could continue in his absence but not wanting to begin an argument that might smoulder for days between them. He'd been looking forward to a romantic interlude at the seaside, not a squabble over her ex-husband.

'All right,' he said, managing a smile. 'At least he's not going to follow you down here, is he?'

'I wouldn't be too sure.'

'Oh no?' This was getting beyond a joke. 'Well, I'll have a thing or two to say to him if he does.'

But she was shaking her head.

'I haven't told you everything yet.'

'So tell me then.'

She hesitated, then said, 'He's obsessed with the idea that you've taken me away from him.'

Harry gave a snort of derision.

'Oh, it's ridiculous, I know it is. I'd already left him before I met you. But I think he's got it into his head that I'd have gone back to him if you hadn't come along. He's . . . well, he's obsessed — that's the only way I can describe it.'

'All right, so he's obsessed. So what?'

'He keeps saying he wants his revenge. Revenge on you.'

The unexpected threat, with its hint of violence, was oddly

reassuring. Harry had been threatened before — and by professionals — and lived to tell the tale. He wouldn't lose much sleep over Greg's wild fantasies.

He laughed. 'So what does he want me to do — lie down so that he can walk all over me?'

She looked at him pityingly. 'He's a lot cleverer than you're giving him credit for.'

He shrugged. He'd known a lot of clever men whose ideas of revenge weren't clever at all but came down to the breaking of bones and spilling of blood. What did clever Greg have in mind that was so different?

'I told you he's a newspaper reporter, didn't I?'

'Yes.'

'He's putting together an article on you.'

His confidence took a sudden jolt. A contract on him — that he might have understood and taken precautions against. An article was somehow less conventional and more sinister.

'A newspaper article about me?'

'Yes.'

'Saying what?'

'Well, from what I can gather, it's going to argue that there should be a licensing system for private detectives. So as to keep out the undesirables. People with criminal records.'

'Like me.'

'You'll be his main example, yes. In fact, his only example. It's going to be a case of Would You Trust This Man With Your Secrets?'

'And will they print it?'

'He seemed to think they'd lap it up.'

Harry gave a grunt of dismay and moved across to stare out of the window, not wanting her to see his face while he adjusted to her news. The thought of Greg the avenger was no longer a joke; publicity such as this would close the agency forever.

'And you talked to him about it?' he said finally.

'I was trying to persuade him not to do it.'

'But he wouldn't listen?'

'No.'

He understood now why she'd wanted him out of the way. Not so much to leave her with a free hand as to stop him killing Greg when he heard the lengths to which the man's malice could take him.

'I'm sorry, Harry,' she said.

'The man's a bastard,' he muttered.

'Oh, I know. I found out the hard way.'

'It'll close the firm. It's bound to. Who the hell's going to want to use us after all that?'

'I know.'

'He'd just better keep well clear of me if he goes ahead with this. Because if it's revenge he wants . . . well, two can play at that game!'

He was beginning to shout and caught sight of himself in the mirror, red-faced and angry. Jill rose from where she was sitting on the bed.

'It's my fault, I know.'

'No.'

'It is.'

'All right then, it is! If that's what you want me to say, well, all right then, it's your fault.'

He regretted his words immediately, wanting to snatch them back.

'Do you want me to go?' she said.

'No.'

'I'd understand if you did.'

'Then he would have won, wouldn't he?' said Harry bitterly.

She said nothing but sat down on the bed again. The silence lengthened. It was becoming dark both outside and in. Harry switched on the light.

'Let's not be stupid,' he said. 'Have you eaten?'

She shook her head.

'Neither have I.'

They went to a Chinese restaurant called the Ming Hoo. Harry ordered sweet-and-sour prawns with fried rice and Jill the Ming Hoo duck special. He took her hand and, for the first time since they'd met that evening, they both managed to smile at the same instant.

'How's the decorating going?' he asked.

'Oh, all right. I'd be enjoying it if it wasn't for Greg and his nasty tricks. I am sorry, Harry.'

'Don't be,' he said, feeling calmer if no less helpless. 'It's not your fault.'

'Oh, isn't it, though?'

'No,' he insisted.

'It's because of me he's doing it. Because we've started living together.'

'So? You think I'd rather we hadn't? Listen, Greg can write what he likes, he can close the business, he can do anything — so long as he doesn't drive you out.'

The food arrived. As usual, Jill asked for chop-sticks while Harry was content with his knife and fork. Gently, not wanting to upset her again, he questioned her about exactly what it was that Greg had first said to her and then what she had said to him. Her account only confirmed what she'd said earlier: that the man was a bastard. He was also a well-established journalist who'd have the skill to do an efficient hatchet-job and then the contacts to sell it. He was out to ruin Harry and make Jill feel she was responsible. All this he'd explained to her in the clearest of terms; then offered her the option of returning to him as the price of his silence.

'What will you do?' she asked.

He shrugged. 'What can I do?'

'I was afraid you might try and find him. To . . . well, to threaten him.'

'No,' he said. It wasn't that it hadn't crossed his mind; just that this was one case where he had to box clever. 'There wouldn't be much point. It'd only give him more to write about.'

He could do nothing but pray that Greg would be knocked down by a double-decker bus or the article run foul of a printers' strike.

They came out of the restaurant to a starry night.

'You fancy a walk?' he asked.

'Love one,' she said, tucking her arm into his. 'Are you going to show me the sights?'

'Well, there aren't all that many. Especially at this time of night. There's the sea over there. Tide's out at the moment but presumably it'll come back. And that's the pier. And that dirty great building more or less across from it — that's the Winter Gardens where the arcade is.'

'Oh yes, how's the case going? I'm sorry, I should have asked.'

'Well, I've discovered something, but I don't know whether it's important or not.'

'Tell me.'

'About three years ago planning permission was granted to turn the place into a casino.'

'So the building might be worth a lot more than it looks,' she said, seeing the consequences immediately.

'Yes. But that's as far as I've got. I haven't established any connection between that and all the other things that've been happening.' And he brought her up to date on the harassment the arcade had suffered, including the minor incident when he himself had been photographed for no apparent reason.

'That'd be Greg,' she said.

He stopped walking and turned to her. 'You think so?'

'Well, probably not him personally. He'd have sent a photographer to get some pictures to go with the article.'

Of course, yes. It made too much sense for her to be wrong. And how would he look in the pictures? Standing next to a rack of dirty post-cards, trying unsuccessfully to duck away from the camera. Just like the shifty ex-con the article would be describing. Perfect really.

Still, at least it was one mystery fewer for him to puzzle over.

'You see,' he said, when they'd resumed walking, 'you've only been here a couple of hours and you're solving my problems for me.'

'I wish I could solve Greg.'

'Look, I vote we don't mention Greg any more tonight. He's done enough damage as it is.'

'Not compared to what that article's going to do.'

'Jill . . .' he pleaded.

'Sorry, sorry, sorry,' she said. 'I swear I won't mention him again. Cross my heart and hope to die.'

They had come to the Winter Gardens, its frontage now dark and shuttered.

'Pity it's not still a dance-hall,' she said. 'You've never taken me dancing.'

'You wouldn't like it if I did. I dance like an elephant.'

She gave a groan of mock-dismay. 'You're a barbarian. You can't dance. You can't do anything. Here, I'll teach you.'

And, under her direction, they side-stepped and shuffled their way along the promenade and then to the door of Floribunda itself. He used his key to open it, then they tiptoed their way up the four flights of stairs, giggling every time a step creaked. Until at last they reached the attic bedroom and their holiday as Harry had foreseen it finally began.

An hour later, the tide started to turn. The waves running towards the darkened beach no longer faltered and fell back but ran on until their impetus was spent. Behind them the deeper water followed.

On it rode the body of a man, fully clothed but inert and lifeless. He pitched backward and forward as the waves ran beneath him, though all the time drifting in towards the beach. He bumped up against the pier supports and stuck there for a moment before another wave arrived to pull him free. Further waves nudged him inch by tantalising inch till he reached the shallows and came to rest on the beach.

Still the water played around him, first threatening to claw him back, then pushing him further ashore as though it couldn't decide whether to have done with him or not. Dawn was beginning to break before the water began its retreat and finally abandoned the body along with the other flotsam and jetsam that fringed the high-water mark along the beach.

7

Breakfast at Floribunda was a hushed and regimented affair served by a waif-like girl called Mary while, it was to be imagined, Mrs Melling operated back-stage in the kitchen. Having the furthest to descend, Harry and Jill were the last to take their places and were greeted by muttered good mornings and stares of curiosity.

Both felt their spirits restored by the night together. The threat posed by Greg's article seemed further off and less potent amid the clatter of cutlery and the smell of egg and bacon.

'I'll take you to see the arcade,' said Harry. 'We'll get Rose to tell your fortune.'

'No, thank you. I'd rather not know. And, anyway, aren't you supposed to be incognito? I don't want to give the game away.'

'It was given away before I'd arrived,' he said, and told her about the reception he'd received.

She laughed. 'That must have been a blow.'

'It was at first. But I'm glad of it now. I don't think I'm cut out to be an actor.'

'But wasn't the idea to find out if any of the arcade staff were involved in all the funny business?'

'Well, yes. But I'm sure they're not.'

'Oh yes?'

'Well, there are only three of 'em. One's the gypsy fortune-teller. Then there's a young lad who I suppose is smart enough for it, but then he was the one the gang of yobboes were setting about so I suppose that sort of puts him in the clear.'

Mary arrived with their egg and bacon so that he had to hurry to shovel down the last of his cereal. Jill had barely touched hers and now pushed it aside.

'And who's the third?'

'Oh, that's old Reg. He was the one that tipped me the wink about the casino angle. I can't see anybody using him as a mole. Not unless they were really desperate.'

'They sound a motley crew.'

'Oh, they're all right. You'll like 'em.'

Or will you, he thought. He still often failed to anticipate her reactions and had been careful to steer her away from most of his old cronies.

They concentrated on eating. Out in the hallway the telephone began to ring.

'I've brought lots of reading,' she said. 'I thought I'd plonk myself in a deck-chair and work through next year's A-level texts.'

'I've been trying to get through that book you gave me.'

'Oh, *Brighton Rock*. What d'you think?'

'Well, it's a bit, er . . .' He didn't have her facility for instant opinions. 'I like it, yes. Just . . . I can't see why they all tag along with that seventeen-year-old kid. I don't know why he killed the man at the beginning either.' One or two heads turned at the talk of killing; Harry's words had intruded upon the chatter about the weather and what to do for the day. 'But it's a good book,' he asserted loudly lest there should be any misunderstanding. 'I'm enjoying it, yes.'

Mrs Melling had appeared and, ignoring the offered smiles and greetings of her other guests, came directly to Harry so that he looked up, startled.

'There's a telephone-call for you, Mr Sommers,' she said. It was almost a rebuke.

'For me? Oh right, thanks.'

She sailed from the room. Harry put down his knife and fork and pulled a face of surprise at Jill.

'Can't think who that can be.'

'Well, it's not me. Not this time.'

'No. Shan't be a minute.'

He came out into the hallway, where the receiver had been left lying on top of the coin-box.

'Hello?' he said, having quickly decided that it would be Yvonne, with news about the Gaming Board or something that'd cropped up at the agency.

'Harry?'

Not Yvonne. It was a man's voice that it took him a moment to identify.

'Derek. How are you?'

'Have you not heard then?'

'Heard what?'

'Nick's dead.' Then, when Harry didn't respond: 'Nick Wyatt, the young man that works for me . . .'

'Yes.'

'He's dead. They found his body this morning.'

'Oh Christ,' said Harry, stunned. 'That's terrible.'

'You're not kidding.'

'Well . . . what's happened? An accident?'

'He's been shot.'

'Shot . . . ?'

'Somebody shot him, then dumped his body in the sea. It landed up on the beach right across from the arcade, would you believe it. Some old geezer out with his dog found him. They thought he'd drowned at first but no, he'd been shot.'

So the climax had been reached then. The awful, logical next step in the escalation of hostilities which had started with the super-glue, the stink-bombs, the messing with the electrics and the visit of the cement-truck, then become more ominous with the arrival of the undertakers and downright dangerous with the attack by the four yobboes, had been taken. Murder. Nick Wyatt, whom Harry had been learning to like and trust, had been killed.

I failed him, thought Harry. I was brought in to sort out the aggro and now look.

'And who . . . I mean does anybody know who did it?' he asked.

'I don't think so. If they do, they're not letting on.'

'And he was shot at the arcade, was he?'

'Oh no. No, they reckon it was a mile or two up the coast. I suppose they can work it out from the way the tide was running, I don't know. Anyway, look, the police want to speak to you. I mean not just you — they want to speak to us all.'

'Yes.'

'Only I had to tell them about you being a private detective and everything.'

'Yes, well, course you did.'

'I said you'd be coming down to the arcade.'

'Oh, right. I'll come now then, shall I?'

'I think you'd better, yes.'

'I'll be there in ten minutes,' he said, and put down the phone.

He stood a moment, composing himself, then went back into the dining-room, where people were finishing their breakfasts and moving away from the tables.

'Everything all right?' Jill asked.

'Tell you in a minute,' he said, wanting not to be overheard this time. He started to eat, surprised he could manage it, and only when they'd been left alone amid the debris of plates and cups and jars of marmalade did he tell her.

The arcade shutters had been opened, revealing an interior that was gloomy and shabby without its lights and music. Harry stepped inside and saw that Derek Underhill was at the far end talking to two men whose demeanour would have betrayed them to be police even if the occasion hadn't.

He'd left Jill at the boarding-house, not knowing what arrangements to make or when he'd be free to meet her. She'd been alarmed by the news, thinking first not of the victim, whom she hadn't known, but of Harry's own involvement.

'Why should the police want to see you?'

'Well, I've been working there. I knew him.'

'They don't suspect you, do they?'

'I suppose they have to suspect everybody.' To forestall further alarm, he added quickly, 'But I've got the perfect alibi, haven't I?'

'What?'

'You. All night.'

'Oh, yes,' she said in a small voice. It seemed to make it worse, not better, that she, too, had a part to play in this charade of violence.

'Don't worry,' he said. 'It's routine. They have to do it.'

'You don't know any more than you've already told me?' she asked him earnestly.

He returned her gaze. 'I wish I did. Then I might have saved the poor kid.'

There was no need to ask where the body had been found. Yards of fluttering tape marked off an area of promenade and beach close to the pier and, as Derek Underhill had said, virtually across the road from the Winter Gardens. There were police-cars parked nearby and a line of shirt-sleeved officers was about to begin a search of the sand. A crowd of holiday-makers stood watching, some faces made solemn by the proximity of death, others unable to suppress a smile at this dramatic bonus to their week.

'This is Harry Sommers, the gentleman I was telling you about,' said Derek as Harry approached.

'I'm Detective-Superintendent Charlton,' said the older of the two policemen. 'And this is Detective-Sergeant Greer.'

Harry nodded.

'And I believe you're a private detective?'

'Yes.'

'Well, let's hope you can help us then.'

Was he being sarcastic? It didn't sound it and no-one was smiling.

'I wish I could,' said Harry.

'Terrible business,' said Derek. 'They ought to bring back hanging, that's what they ought to do.'

'I think I'd like to talk to you down at the station, Mr Sommers,' said the Superintendent. 'Sergeant Greer'll take you along. You've no objections I hope?'

'No.'

Should he have had? Too late now anyway. Sergeant Greer said, 'Come on then,' and headed for the door. Harry followed, past the rows of silent one-arm bandits and blank space invader machines.

They crossed the promenade and went to one of the police-cars. Those of the crowd nearest to the car turned and watched with interest as Harry climbed in. Reading their faces, he thought, they're wondering if I'm being arrested, wondering if I'm the one who shot him.

The interview room brought back uncomfortable memories of the others he'd occupied when, first as juvenile, then as adult, he'd broken Her Majesty's law and been done for it. The petty theft had taken him as far as the magistrates' court; the later offences of causing an affray and assault had taken him a good deal further, to Wormwood Scrubs where he'd served a total of nine months.

But always, along the way, there'd been rooms like this, functional and masculine, designed to make you feel uneasy and trapped.

Though this time, of course, he wasn't trapped. He was there of his own free will to offer what help he could towards the solving of a crime committed by someone else. He could ask the constable for a cup of tea if he wanted one and have a wander down the corridor as far as the toilets whenever he liked. Sergeant Greer popped in a couple of times to apologise for the delay. It seemed they were waiting for Superintendent Charlton to return.

Or was that a trick? All part of the process? You could never know for sure. All he did know was that, two hours and one cup of tea later, he was still waiting. What would Jill be thinking?

What would she be doing? And suppose they'd fed his name into the police-computer — which they must have done by now — what interesting food for thought would that have provided, with full details of his pock-marked past? They'd soon have discovered this was no ordinary, law-abiding private detective they'd got on their hands, but the black sheep of his profession.

It was a small surprise, then, to have Superintendent Charlton arrive full of apologies rather than accusations. There'd been a lot to see to, he explained; they were unaccustomed to murder in St Stephen's Bay.

He was a big man, older and heavier than Harry, with receding hair and a spreading gut. He had about him a disarming air of patience that suggested he wouldn't be hurried but no more would he be shaken off. On this occasion he took off his jacket, wiped his brow with his handkerchief, rolled up his sleeves, retrieved a box of matches and packet of cigarettes from the pocket of his jacket, placed them side by side on the table, sent for two cups of tea, and only then asked his first question.

'Do you own a gun?'

Despite the time he'd had to prepare himself, it took Harry by surprise.

'Me?'

'Well, you're a private detective. I'm sure some of you chaps must be licensed to carry arms.'

'Oh, well, no. I'm not.'

'Just wondering. What were you doing yesterday evening?'

'Well, I was at the arcade till about half-seven and then I walked along to the railway station to meet, er . . . to meet a young lady who was joining me from London.'

'And what time did she arrive?'

'Oh, about half-eight. Her train was late because of the fog.'

'Who is this young lady?'

'Her name's Jill Hanscome. We live together in London.' Only just, but it was true all the same.

'You went to meet her at half-past-seven and her train didn't arrive till half-past-eight. . . . ?'

'Yes.'

'It can't have taken you an hour to walk from the arcade to the station. More like ten minutes I'd say.'

Harry shrugged. 'I had a cup of coffee. Hung about. I didn't know how late the train was going to be.'

'And you were by yourself all this time?'

'Yes.'

'Hmmm. Only the doctor's preliminary examination suggests that time of death was between half-seven and half-eight yesterday evening.'

Harry said nothing. He had the feeling things were going from bad to worse and wasn't sure what to do to stop the rot. He tried a modest counter-atack.

'I didn't kill him if that's what you're getting at.'

'No?'

'No.'

'So who did?'

'I haven't a clue.'

'Well, you've had longer on the case than we've had. We've had little more than three hours where you've had three days.'

'It wasn't the same case,' said Harry evenly.

'Don't you think so?'

'I wasn't brought here to investigate murder.'

'Oh, I know why you were brought here. I've talked to Mr Underhill and heard all about his little problems. Which, I may say, he didn't see fit to inform us about.'

Harry maintained a tactful silence.

'Anyway, don't you think there might be a connection? All those bits of bother — getting more and more serious — and now this . . . ?'

'There might be.'

'I know there might be. Do you think there is?'

'Probably, yes.'

'So do I. So. Did you make any progress in sorting out what was going on?'

'Not really.'

'You spend three days on a case and you're still no wiser than if you'd stayed at home in Bermondsey or wherever it is?'

It was all said quite calmly, without overt sarcasm or scorn. But it rankled with Harry, as doubtless it was meant to.

'Oh, I wouldn't say that.'

'No?'

'No.' He hesitated but, having made the call, he now had to show his hand. 'For one thing, I found out that planning permission was granted three years ago to turn the Winter Gardens into a casino.'

Superintendent Charlton thought about it, then said, 'And is that important?'

'I just wondered if somebody might be trying to force Derek Underhill out of the building.'

Another thoughtful pause from the Superintendent, then: 'Interesting idea. Who, though?'

'I don't know.' Then, feeling he hadn't told the full story, he added, 'By the way, it wasn't Derek Underhill who made the application. It was Charlie Monroe.'

'Monroe . . . ?'

'You know him?'

'Of course I know him. I'd have to be blind, deaf and dumb not to. So he was the one with the big ideas for a casino, then.'

'It looks like it.'

'Fascinating. But does it get us any nearer to who shot Nicholas Wyatt?'

'That wasn't what I was investigating at the time,' Harry reminded him.

'No, of course you weren't. But it's what we're all doing now.'

'Yes.'

'What about those Hell's Angels that raided the place?'

'Hell's Angels . . . ?' echoed Harry, mystified for a moment.

'I was talking to the other attendant and he was saying . . .'

'Oh yes,' said Harry, realising. 'But they weren't Hell's Angels, no. Just four yobboes in leather jackets and helmets. They looked as if they'd come in with the idea of creating bother.'

'They were going for the lad that's been shot, were they?'

'Well, only because he tried to stop them tipping over one of the pin-tables. I don't think it was personal.'

'Would you recognise any of them again?'

'I doubt it.'

'Has anybody threatened you while you've been here?'

'No.'

'Nobody tried to warn you off?'

Harry started to shake his head, then said, 'Well, there was something . . . though it didn't seem serious. . . .'

'What?'

'Well, I'd hardly set foot in the place before two undertakers turned up. Somebody had told 'em I was dead.'

'Sounds serious to me.'

'I just thought it was part of the aggravation that was going on. Somebody had phoned and given my name.'

'Somebody who knew you were coming.'

'Must have done.'

'And how many people knew that?'

'Well, Derek Underhill of course. And Charlie Monroe. I'd worked for him once before and he'd sort of recommended me.'

'Funny how that name keeps cropping up, isn't it?'

'I think word had got around generally, though,' said Harry quickly, lest he should seem to be pointing the finger at Charlie. 'The three that worked in the arcade, they all knew what I was doing there.'

The Superintendent took out a cigarette, lit it, then said, 'And what about Nicholas Wyatt then? What did you make of him?'

'Well, he was a bit of a Jack-the-lad if you know what I mean.'

'Tell me.'

'Well, he was bright enough, fancied himself, not settled or anything like that.'

'Was he on the fiddle?'

'No,' said Harry, then wondered how he could sound so certain. 'Well, if he was then I saw nothing of it.'

'Did he ever give you the impression he had enemies?'

Harry thought about it, then slowly shook his head. 'He was a friendly, easy-going sort of lad. Though he'd let you know if there was something he didn't like.'

'He let you know, did he?'

'Well, relations were a bit strained to start with 'cause they all three resented me being there. They thought I was checking up on 'em.'

'They were right then, weren't they?'

'I suppose so.'

'And you found nothing.'

'Only what I've already said.'

'About Charlie Monroe and his planning permission. Yes, it's very interesting, that. I won't forget about that, you needn't worry. By the way, did you ever ask him about it?'

'Not Charlie, no.'

'Why not?'

'Well . . . just never got round to it.'

'You said he recommended you. That you used to work for him.'

'He once employed me in a club he was running. Up in London.'

'A place in Twickenham, was it?'

Harry looked at him in surprise. 'Yes.'

'Address was seventy-two Millicent Road. Joint proprietors were Charlie Monroe and a Mr M. Baxter.'

Harry could only nod, taken aback by the extent of his information.

The Superintendent allowed himself a smile. 'You see, it's true what they say about these computers. Pretty soon we'll know everything about everybody. And won't that make life easier?'

'Easier for some.'

'Exactly.'

Harry waited to be told about his own convictions and spells of imprisonment but that never came. The Superintendent, having demonstrated the omniscience of the computer, seemed content to leave it at that and let Harry conclude for himself that if they knew so much about the club in Twickenham then they'd certainly know all about him.

'He wasn't on drugs, was he, this Nicholas Wyatt?'

'Not that I ever noticed.'

'And would you have noticed?'

'Perhaps not,' admitted Harry. 'But if he was then it didn't show.'

'Did he ever say anything about his family?'

'Not to me.'

'Did he have a girlfriend?'

'I don't know. He never mentioned anybody in particular.'

'Did you ever see him with a girl?'

'No.' Then, fearing he was in danger of misrepresenting Nick, he said, 'But I assumed he was meeting girls when he went off at night.'

'Why should you assume that?'

'Well, he had quite a talent for chatting 'em up in the arcade. I saw him doing that often enough.'

'So he wasn't queer?'

'No chance.'

'It's funny,' said the Superintendent, 'the more I hear about him, the less I can understand why anybody should want to shoot him. I mean there he is — young, good-looking, quite a charmer when he wants to be, honest employee, no ties, footloose and fancy-free . . . then things start going wrong in the arcade and suddenly he's dead. Why?'

'I wish I could tell you,' said Harry, suddenly bitter. 'And I hope you catch the bastard that did it.'

The Superintendent observed Harry but said nothing. He stubbed out his cigarette.

'What about the other attendant, what's his name . . . ?'

'Reg Smith.'

'How did Nick get on with him?'

'Oh, he used to take the mickey a bit. You know what young lads are like.'

'Used to get the old man riled, did he?'

Seeing the implications of the question, Harry felt bound to protest: 'Not so that he'd want to kill him if that's what you mean. No, they got on all right really. It was just a game between 'em.'

The Superintendent nodded. 'And what about the gypsy woman?'

Harry could only shrug. He hadn't really got to know Rose. Nick and she had seemed friendly enough. What could he say?

'You scratch a gypsy, you generally find a rogue underneath,' mused the Superintendent. 'Did any of her family ever use to hang around the place?'

'None that I ever saw.'

The door opened and Sergeant Greer entered. He didn't look at Harry but placed a typewritten sheet of paper in front of the Superintendent.

'Post-mortem report,' he said, then stood and waited while the Superintendent glanced through it.

Poor Nick, thought Harry. The typewritten sheet had brought with it a sudden vision of the young man cold in the mortuary. Harry felt himself obscurely responsible and wished he could offer more help towards bringing the killer to book.

'Well, it's what we thought,' said the Superintendent at last. 'Shot first, then thrown into the sea. Any idea?'

'Not a lot,' said the Sergeant.

'Well, Mr Sommers and I have had an interesting chat.' He turned to Harry. 'What will you be doing now?'

It was a good question.

'I don't know,' said Harry. 'The idea was I'd be working at the arcade for a couple of weeks but now . . . I'll have to talk to Mr Underhill, see what he wants.'

'Needless to say, we'd like to know if you're planning to leave St Stephen's Bay.'

'Sure.'

'And if you have any more ideas on the case we'd be delighted to hear them.'

It was a relief to escape from the interview room. He was under no illusions and knew they'd check out his every move and perhaps have him in again, but at least he was free for the time being and could go in search of Jill. He'd half-expected to see Reg or Rose waiting their turn to be questioned but the foyer was empty. The constable on duty behind the desk didn't even glance up as he passed.

There was little sign of activity outside either. Obviously all the action was still down at the promenade.

Then, as he came down the steps of the police-station, beneath the word 'POLICE' etched in blue, he noticed a car parked on the opposite side of the road. He'd seen it before somewhere. A camera lens appeared from its lowered front window and suddenly he understood both where he'd seen it and what it was doing parked there now.

It was too late to cover his face — and, anyway, what sort of a picture would that produce? — so he started forward, shouting, 'Hey . . . !' The camera disappeared. He got close enough to see that the man in the car wasn't Greg but a stranger. He made a grab at the door but was too late. The car shot forward with a lurch. All he could manage was to bring his fist down on the boot as it went away from him, making a dent in the metal and splitting one of his knuckles.

8

'Just tell me one thing.'

'What?'

'Is it always going to be like this?'

He thought of feigning ignorance – was what always going to be like what? – but knew all too well what it was Jill was demanding as they sat on deck-chairs staring morosely out to sea. She wanted to know would his life always be dogged by violence or had he, as he constantly reassured her, really broken his links with the unenviable past?

'I didn't know he was going to be killed,' he said quietly.

'No?'

He groaned. 'No. Why, do you think I did?'

She didn't answer but instead came up with a new challenge: 'Could it have happened because you're here?'

'I've no reason for thinking it did.'

'But you do seem to have a talent for being around when things like that happen.'

'It's not one I'm particularly proud of.'

'I'm glad to hear it.'

It had been the visit from the police, checking out his alibi with her, that had plunged her into this mood of anxiety and bitterness. She'd grown up with the middle-class view of the Old Bill as friendly, avuncular figures on bicycles, telling the time and directing foreigners to Harrods. Finding herself the object of their suspicious questioning had been an upsetting experience. And, in an obscure way, it was all Harry's fault.

'Look, I'm sorry you've been dragged in,' he said. 'What do you want? Do you want to go back to London?' When she didn't reply, he persevered: 'If you want to go back we can get you on a train today.'

'Do you want me to go?'

'No.' Another pause. 'Unless you want to.' Then, exasperated by the unfairness of it all, he blurted out, 'Only I can do without the lectures. I mean, for God's sake, I feel bad enough about the lad. I don't need aggro from you as well.'

'I see,' she said.

'Good,' he said, wondering whether he'd blown it and she'd flounce off, leaving St Stephen's Bay on the next train and perhaps their flat in Islington as well.

But she didn't go. They sat side by side without speaking, watching the high tide begin its retreat from the smooth stones of the sea-wall.

'You got tickets?' said a voice. They looked up and saw a ticket-collector standing above them, his machine slung low on his hip. 'Twenty-five pee a chair.' Harry fished out a fifty-pence piece and he reeled off the tickets and moved away.

'I'm sorry,' she said. 'I didn't mean to go on at you.'

He shrugged. 'Doesn't matter.'

'Yes it does. You deserve somebody better than me. Somebody who'll give you some support. Would you really like me to go back to London?'

'What do you think?' he said, light-headed with relief that she was sticking to him, wanting only that things should again be easy between them.

She smiled and took his hand. 'Thanks. I think it's just all been a bit of a shock, that's all.'

'What you need is an ice-lolly.'

But she wanted to be serious. 'I am on your side, Harry. I am really.'

'You'd better be,' he said. ''Cause there aren't that many that are. Now — what flavour?'

Being strictly business, his dealings with Derek Underhill were more straightforward.

'Do you want me to carry on or what?' Harry asked him when they met up after each had been separately grilled by the phlegmatic Superintendent Charlton.

He didn't hesitate. 'I do, yes. That's if you still want to.'

'It's what you're paying me for.'

'Well, not for this kind of thing, I'm not. I wasn't reckoning on 'em coming at us with shooters.'

'You think Nick's death was to do with the arcade?'

'Bit of a coincidence otherwise.'

It occurred to Harry to ask about the two-year-old project to turn the decaying Winter Gardens into a casino but he decided against it. There seemed nothing to be gained. Either it was of no importance or it'd already led to murder. He'd told the police all he knew; let them try and make sense of it.

He remembered a dictum of Clifford Humphries, founder and, till his death, sole proprietor of the agency: 'Do what you're employed for. No more, no less. There are clients who'll have you collecting the laundry and walking the dog if they can get away with it.'

Good advice, and never more relevant than now when he'd come to mind a slot-machine and found he'd let himself in for a good deal more than he'd bargained for. Though still not as much as poor Nick, who'd been pursuing a modest version of the good life — mainly nurses on day trips or shop-girls on their annual holiday — and had ended on a slab in the town's mortuary.

'When are you re-opening?' asked Harry.

'Tomorrow. I'll close again for the funeral of course. But what good will leaving the place locked up do? Won't bring him back, will it?'

News of the murder had swept like a tidal-wave through the tightly-packed rows of hotels and boarding-houses, flowing unchecked from landlady to landlady. It was the biggest single topic of conversation since, in 1973, a Liberal peer had raped the winner of the Miss St Stephen's Bay competition he'd come to judge.

Back at Floribunda, Mrs Melling's attitude towards Harry — never over-enthusiastic — became more complicated. Clearly she still didn't altogether approve of him and his recently-arrived 'wife'; nevertheless his residence under her roof gave her a certain status among her colleagues. She cleaned his room with a particular thoroughness.

It was the morning after the finding of the body before he got round to ringing Yvonne.

'Hello,' he said. 'It's Harry.'

'Everything all right?'

'Not really.' And he told her about the murder.

'Oh my God,' was her first reaction. Then: 'And who do they suspect?'

'Nobody as yet. They've had me in for questioning so don't be surprised if you have somebody round checking up on the agency.'

'And are you staying on?'

'For the time being. See what happens next. If anything does.'

'Oh Harry, do be careful.'

'Don't worry. I intend to be.'

'And who was he, this boy who was shot?'

'Just a kid down from the country. Hadn't an enemy in the world till somebody decided to put a bullet in him.'

'Oh, that's dreadful. Has it been on the news? I didn't see it last night and I haven't read the papers yet.'

'Yes,' said Harry, who hadn't seen it either but who'd been given a word-for-word report by Mrs Melling. 'And there'll be more to come, you can count on it.' Including Greg's piece on himself, he thought, though he said nothing. No point in alarming Yvonne further. Though alarmed, and warned, she'd have to be sooner or later. No doubt the murder had come as a god-send to the muck-raking Greg, just the additional ingredient he needed to give his article on Harry the edge of topicality as well as bolstering the case against him.

'Actually I was on the point of phoning you,' said Yvonne after they'd exhausted the subject of Nick's murder. 'Though I don't know how much it matters now.'

'You've talked to the Gaming Board,' he guessed.

'Yes.'

'Well then, it might matter a hell of a sight more than I ever expected. What did they say?'

'They said there's no chance at all of a casino ever being established in St Stephen's Bay.'

'No . . . ?' Whatever he'd expected, it wasn't this.

'No chance. See, ever since nineteen sixty-eight gambling's been restricted to certain areas. Oh, except for bingo. You can do that anywhere.'

'What areas?'

'Well, there's quite a list. Forty-six of 'em are in England, two in Wales, four in Scotland. You don't want me to read it out, do you?'

He didn't. 'St Stephen's Bay isn't on the list?'

'No.'

'Damn,' he said, seeing his single line of investigation hit a dead-end.

'You can always apply for somewhere new to be added to the list but you'd have to show that it had a big population and no existing casinos anywhere near it.'

Harry thought about the population of St Stephen's Bay. Couldn't be more than forty or fifty thousand. And there were already casinos nearby in Brighton and Bournemouth.

'Does all that help?' asked Yvonne.

'No. I mean yes, it does, thanks. It helps me realise I've been barking up the wrong tree.'

It also explained why Charlie Monroe — with or without the partnership of Derek Underhill — had never pursued the idea of converting the Winter Gardens beyond obtaining planning permission from the local authority. There was nothing sinister about it. Charlie's ambitions must have been sabotaged by the rules and regulations of the Gaming Board. They'd said no and that had been the end of it.

Save that hot-shot private investigator Harry Sommers had come along two years later and, acting on information given him by the unreliable and ill-informed Reg Smith, had thrown himself headlong into a series of false assumptions.

'Did you mention St Stephen's Bay?' he asked forlornly.

'Yes. They said it didn't seem a likely area for permission to be given. I even asked if they'd ever been approached about it but they wouldn't answer that. Said all such applications were treated in strictest confidence.'

Harry promised to keep in touch and rang off, remembering just too late that he hadn't asked her how she was managing with the agency's other cases. Probably better than he was with his solitary one. He was dispirited by what she'd had to tell him, wondering suddenly whether there was any point in staying on or whether he might not cut his own losses, and Derek Underhill's bill, by abandoning the case.

The arcade re-opened with Derek himself taking a turn in the change booth now they were short-staffed. Across the promenade the red tapes placed by the police to mark off the site where the body was found had already been removed. Life was returning to what passed as normal — families on the beach, couples strolling arm-in-arm. The arcade was busier than ever with gawping holiday-makers attracted by its new notoriety.

Also attracted were Superintendent Charlton and Sergeant Greer who wandered in during the afternoon. While the Superintendent chatted to Derek, the Sergeant approached Harry. The two men exchanged nods of recognition.

'All quiet on the western front?' asked the Sergeant.

'Seems to be.'

'Good.'

Harry waited, sensing rightly that there was more to come.

'I was thinking about the various problems you were having before the murder.'

'Yes?'

'Didn't one of them involve somebody tampering with the power-supply? Reducing the voltage so as to send the machines haywire?'

'That was before I got here,' said Harry defensively.

'Oh, I know. It was Underhill who told us about it. Only what I was thinking, see — that must have been an inside job, mustn't it? Must have been done by somebody who could get access.'

Harry shrugged. He'd considered that himself but hadn't known what conclusions to draw. It might once have pointed the finger at Nick, but surely now he was well beyond suspicion.

Or was he? Sergeant Greer seemed prepared to think ill of the dead.

'I was wondering whether it might have been Nick Wyatt doing it, whether there might have been somebody putting him up to it . . . ? What do you think?'

'I can't see it,' said Harry, shaking his head. 'What about the four yobboes that set about him?'

'Maybe that was to give him an alibi, put him in the clear.'

'And then what? He shot himself and threw himself into the sea?'

He hadn't meant it to sound as scornful as it did — just that he felt protective about Nick, who'd been a tragic victim of the whole charade and surely deserved better than to be thought of as its perpetrator.

But Sergeant Greer seemed not to mind. 'Just an idea,' he said cheerily. 'We're a bit short of 'em at the moment.'

Superintendent Charlton moved to join them.

'All right, Mr Sommers?'

'Yes.'

'We checked up on your casino idea. It was the Gaming Board

put the mockers on it. Otherwise this place would've been worth a fortune.'

'I see,' said Harry shortly. He'd already had his mistake explained to him by Yvonne and could do without a repeat. 'Sorry I was wasting your time.'

'Oh, you weren't, no. Let us know if you've any more notions like that. You never know what one of 'em might lead to. Anyway, we'll be off then.'

'You might have mentioned it, Harry,' said Derek reproachfully as the two officers left. He'd been close enough to overhear their conversation. 'I mean you might have told me what you were thinking about the casino and everything. I could have marked your card for you.'

'I was going to. Till this business with Nick, then it sort of slipped my mind.'

'It's just I don't think Charlie'd like it if he found out his name was being mentioned.'

It irritated Harry that, faced with Nick's murder, he was expected to think of Charlie Monroe and his tender feelings.

'I don't see why that should worry him.'

'Well, they was asking me about him.'

'So what did you tell 'em?'

'Well, the truth. What else? Charlie and me had this idea about setting the old place back on its feet again as a casino. We checked out the local angle. No problems. They were as delighted as I was to think this flea-bitten old monument might be put to some use. So then Charlie goes to the Gaming Board but they aren't having any of it. They tell him there's more than enough casinos around here as it is, so we can forget it.'

'That's a shame,' said Harry, 'but I don't see that the cops knowing that does Charlie any harm.'

'I'm just thinking about it from his point of view. Him and the police don't always see eye to eye. They'd probably welcome the excuse to turn him over.'

'He'll survive it,' said Harry irritably.

103

Amazing how quickly sympathy for the dead and the wish for justice became qualified by the self-interest of the living. Find Nick Wyatt's murderer, was the cry — but be careful whose toes you tread on in the process.

He met Jill that evening and they went for a meal at a sea-front restaurant specialising in Japanese cooking.

'How's the reading going?' he asked.

'Not as well as it should. It's too much of a temptation just to sit back in the sun.'

She had the beginnings of a tan and seemed calmer than before. He decided to broach the topic uppermost in his mind: when was Greg likely to put pen to paper and cause the sword suspended over Harry's own head to fall?

'Did Greg say when this article about me's likely to appear?'

She didn't seem surprised that he should be thinking of it and answered immediately.

'No. Just as soon as he can manage it, I suppose.'

'They got another picture of me. As I was coming out of the police-station. So that should look good. Private detective released after helping police with their enquiries.' He gave a hollow laugh.

'Was it Greg who took it?'

'No. Some bloke I've never seen before.'

She fell silent and, fearing he'd depressed her by his talk about Greg, he tried to strike a cheerful note. 'Still, no point in worrying about it. Nothing either of us can do. Let's eat, drink and be merry, eh.' And he attacked with gusto the seaweed-like concoction Jill had ordered for them both.

But he needn't have worried: rather than brooding, she was considering a new angle. 'I wonder if the murder might have stopped him. At least for the time being.'

The seaweed was proving difficult to chew. 'How d'you mean?' he asked through it.

'Well, so long as there's a chance you might be involved in Nick Wyatt's murder—' she put up a quick hand before he could protest —'I mean as far as they know. In fact, as far as they know, you could end up being charged with it.'

'Let's hope they're wrong.'

'Yes, but what I'm saying – perhaps they daren't publish anything about you till someone's been charged with the murder. In case it does turn out to be you and then they'd have prejudiced opinion against you.'

It was an interesting idea. And a relief to feel he might have been granted a stay of execution. Albeit at such a dreadful cost.

'So poor old Nick's got me off the hook.'

'I would think he has, yes. And if you were actually to go ahead and solve the case . . .'

'Then it'd be a miracle.'

'It might be. But it'd also make you the hero of the hour. And then not even Greg could sell an article knocking you. Not if you'd beaten the police to it and found their murderer.'

Harry gave a grunt of agreement, though he didn't feel much encouraged. So that was all he had to do, was it? Play Sherlock Holmes, unmask the villain and leave the flatfoots of the local force gasping in admiration.

'Can't you think of an easier way?' he asked with a small smile.

'Only me doing what Greg wants and going back to him.'

'No,' he said, meaning that wouldn't be easier; that would be unthinkable. 'I'd better solve the murder then, hadn't I?'

The meal over, they strolled back along the promenade towards the Winter Gardens. It was nine o'clock. The arcade would still be open and he thought it his duty to check that nothing untoward had occurred during his absence. It was another gloriously warm evening, tempting drinkers to bring their pints and Babychams out on to the pavements till there was a small crowd outside each public house and the window-sills were full of empty glasses. The newsagent next to the arcade still displayed its rack of dirty post-cards. Jill stopped to examine them. Harry glanced round apprehensively, remembering it was here he'd first been snapped by Greg's photographer.

'Oh, look at these,' she exclaimed.

He looked, and saw again the fat man with his little Willie and the nudist with her broken G-string. Expecting Jill to comment on their vulgarity, he was surprised when she said, 'Aren't they marvellous.'

'Are they?'

'Yes. They're by Donald McGill.'

'You know him?'

'No. Oh, we must get some. We can stick them up in the kitchen.'

'If you like.'

She saw his puzzlement and explained: 'They're almost collector's pieces. The originals are worth a fortune.'

He tried to look interested as she selected half-a-dozen and went into the shop to pay for them. He should have been used by now to her preference for anything quaint or tacky – old sewing-machine bases or chipped statuettes – while everything he thought smart and attractive made her wince in disapproval.

The arcade had quietened down, with just a few punters left to play the bandits and the pin-tables. Reg had the evening off and so Gypsy Rose had stayed on to help Derek lock up.

'You seen the paper?' said Derek, as Harry and Jill entered.

'No,' said Harry in alarm, thinking of Greg's plans to discredit him.

Derek tossed him a folded copy of the evening paper.

'Bottom of the front page.'

'Inquest on Local Man Adjourned' read Harry, to his relief. It was an account of the inquest on Nick. There'd been nothing new or unexpected: a statement by the witness who'd found the body; the results of the post mortem; a report by the police. He passed the paper over to Jill.

'Nothing happened here?' he asked Derek.

'Nothing out of the ordinary. Some snotty-nosed kid was sick on the helicopter but I don't suppose anybody could have planned that, could they?'

'You got a minute, Harry?' said a voice at his elbow.

He turned and found Gypsy Rose who, being off-duty, had removed her shawl and brass ear-rings.

'Sure.'

'Something I want to talk to you about,' she said. 'We'll go next door, shall we?'

'Yes,' he said, surprised and made curious by her sudden wish to confide in him. Of the arcade's personnel, she was the one he knew least.

He told Jill where he was going, then followed Gypsy Rose through the curtained doorway of her booth. Inside was lit by a single red bulb; the walls displayed faded photographs of the once-famous who'd crossed her palm. The crystal ball lay on the table between them till she pushed it aside. They weren't talking about the future then.

'Something I want to tell you about Nick,' she began abruptly.

'Yes?'

'Only I didn't want to tell the coppers. And I don't suppose they'd take any notice if I did.'

No need to ask why. Though no gypsy, Harry had grown up in a community that didn't readily confide in the police, but regarded them as the sharp end of all hostile authority. Rose might have stopped travelling but her old allegiances and prejudices remained.

'You know something about why he was killed?'

'Not for certain. All I do know is that he'd got himself involved in something that he was all secretive about. Something that'd been going on for a week or two before you arrived.'

'Like what?'

She shrugged. 'I don't know exactly. It's just the way he was acting.' She sensed Harry's disappointment at her vagueness and added, 'You learn to weigh people up in this game, dear. That's where the skill lies. And it's a real gift, whatever people might think.'

'I'm sure it is,' said Harry sincerely.

'Well then, I knew Nick. He was a good boy. And he didn't have any family here or anybody else very close and so he used to talk to me. Tell me things. About his girlfriends, that sort of thing. Then a few weeks ago he came over all mysterious. Like there was something he was pleased about but that had to remain a big secret.'

'But you don't know what it was?'

She shook her head. 'I'd have said it was a girl — somebody special — except that he normally told me about his young ladies. He was quite a Romeo was our Nick,' she added sadly.

Harry nodded but felt at a bit of a loss. He didn't doubt Rose's reading of the situation — as she said, she was a professional. But when she'd started talking he'd hoped for something specific, something that might have given him the chance he needed to at least contribute to bringing the killer to book. It wasn't just Jill's suggestion that he might yet upstage Greg's article by cracking the case ahead of the police; he owed it to Nick to do all he could.

'There was just one thing,' she said.

'What?'

'An address he'd written down and that I just happened to catch sight of.'

There was a touch of defiance about her announcement: he could think her nosey or interfering if he wished. But he was only excited to find she'd been saving the best till last and might, after all, have something concrete to offer him.

'And you think this address is connected to . . . well, to whatever it was he had going for him?'

'Well, I certainly wasn't meant to see it. He was in the back office, talking on the phone, and rang off as soon as he saw me. Then Derek wanted him and he went out leaving this scrap of paper he'd been writing on. Two minutes later he was back for it, but I'd seen it by then.'

'Can you remember the address?'

Rose smiled. No doubt remembering bits and pieces was another facet of her strange profession.

'Twenty-one Salmon Gardens,' she recited.

'Twenty-one Salmon Gardens,' repeated Harry. 'And you haven't told this to the police?'

'No. Never asked me, did they? And, anyhow, they've never done me no favours so why should I start doing their job for 'em?'

'Do you know where this is, this Salmon Gardens?'

She shook her head. 'Never heard of it before, dear.'

'And you haven't tried to find out?'

'No. I probably wouldn't even have remembered it if it hadn't been for this dreadful business. It's only because of what happened that I thought it might mean something.'

'OK,' said Harry. 'And thanks. I mean for telling me.'

'Oh, I think I can trust you, dear. Like I say, you learn to weigh people up in this game. I think Nick trusted you eventually.'

'I hope he did,' said Harry.

Walking back to Floribunda with Jill, he felt he'd been offered a second chance when he'd least expected it. And this time there'd be no cock-ups. If 21 Salmon Gardens existed, then he'd find it. With luck — and there hadn't been much of that around lately — it might prove the missing piece of the jigsaw, making sudden sense of a picture that still remained fragmented and baffling.

9

The funeral procession advanced down the promenade at little more than walking pace, passing the Winter Gardens with its closed and shuttered arcade. It was a procession of three cars: a hearse, then a black funeral car carrying three members of Nick's family down from Norwich, and finally Derek Underhill driving his own car with Reg, Gypsy Rose and Harry as passengers.

Its slow progress along the crowded sea-front drew looks of surprise from the assembled holiday-makers, even of annoyance from those who regarded it as a tasteless infringement on their pleasure, something not mentioned in the brochure. Though a few, mainly older people, stood as a mark of respect.

Not much of a send-off, thought Harry, whose last funeral had been that of Johnny Askey, porn racketeer, whom half of Stepney had turned out to see buried. The bronze casket had carried a giant cross of white roses, inscribed 'From the girls'; behind it had walked six greyhounds, favourites of the deceased, and a race-horse called Centre Fold. Then, too, it had been winter and gloomy, a suitable day for a funeral; today was high summer and the beach was full, a cruel mockery of their sad task.

The police, in the unmistakable shape of Messrs Charlton and Greer, were waiting at the entrance to the crematorium. They stayed only till the two cars had disgorged the small group of mourners, then left, apparently satisfied — or disappointed — that there was no-one there they might not have expected.

The service was short, with taped organ music, a reading of 'The Lord is My Shepherd' and a recital of the Lord's Prayer in which all were invited to join. Derek Underhill stood silent throughout; Reg and Rose responded loudly as though in competition; Harry mumbled along. The family from Norwich — a middle-aged couple who must have been his parents and a younger woman who might have been an elder sister — seemed shell-shocked, their eyes never leaving the coffin till it slid away to oblivion. The clergyman conducting the service stepped forward and spoke consolingly to the family in a low voice. Harry slipped thankfully out of the door and into the sunshine.

'Just the gentleman I was looking for.'

He looked in surprise and saw Charlie Monroe coming across the clipped lawn towards him. His Mercedes was parked just inside the crematorium gates.

'All right, Charlie,' said Harry, his voice hushed by the ceremony he'd just witnessed.

But Charlie wasn't all right. . . . Nor had he any inhibitions about saying so at the top of his voice, funeral or no.

'What the hell have you been telling the police about me?'

For a moment Harry thought he was going to be physically attacked and raised his arms in instinctive defence. But Charlie came to an abrupt halt before him and stood glowering. Though shorter than Harry, his rage seemed to lend him extra height. It was all Harry could do to stand his ground, resisting the temptation to step back, away from the other man's fury.

'I didn't know I'd been telling them anything.'

'Oh no? Then why have I had 'em sniffing around? Asking about me and that bloody monstrosity of a building?'

'The Winter Gardens . . . ?'

He knew, of course, what the outburst was all about and might have apologised had Charlie's approach been different. As it was, he could do no more than try and ride out the storm.

'Yes, the Winter bleeding Gardens,' snarled Charlie, 'that nobody in his right mind would want given.'

'Listen, Charlie . . .'

'No, you listen to me, Mr Clever Dick private detective. I got you this job, see. I got you this job 'cause I thought you might appreciate the work. And what happens?'

'I only . . .'

'You only go and tell the Old Bill that I'm behind all the aggravation. You only go pointing the finger at yours truly!'

'I didn't do that.'

'Oh yes.'

'No.'

'Then what're they doing dragging me out of a lunch at the bleeding golf club? Dragging me out in front of everybody who's bleeding anybody round here and half of whom are magistrates and are going to remember it next time I'm applying for a licence. You're lucky I don't arrange to have your arse kicked all the way round this bleeding town!'

The other mourners were now emerging from the crematorium, gazing wide-eyed at the solidly-built, bull-necked man in a light blue cotton suit who was yelling into Harry's face.

'I'm sorry if you've been inconvenienced,' said Harry evenly.

'Inconvenienced . . . ? You bet I've been inconvenienced. And you were the one behind it.'

'They'd have found out anyway.'

'There's nothing to find out.'

'I mean about the application. About the casino idea.'

Charlie sneered. 'Part of your job is it, being copper's nark?'

Harry straightened and his tone took on something of Charlie's belligerence.

'No, it isn't. But it isn't part of my job to lie on your behalf either.'

'Nobody was asking you to.'

'Right. So all I did was tell 'em what I'd heard. What they wanted to make of it, that was their doing, so go and jump up and down on their necks and stay off mine.'

Charlie hesitated, then nodded slowly and put up a warning finger.

'I won't forget this. I owe you one for this.'

'That's not all you owe me,' said Harry. 'I reckon I'm still a hundred quid down on last time I had anything to do with you.'

Charlie stared at him. Behind them the mourners stood in an astonished silence. For a moment they formed a frozen tableau, then Charlie looked past Harry and addressed Derek Underhill.

'Get him out of here. I don't want to see him around, all right?'

He turned on his heel and stomped away towards the Mercedes. Harry's fists were clenched and he was aware of a vein throbbing lightly in his temple.

Derek came forward to stand beside him. He shook his head and gave a sigh of dismay.

'I told you, didn't I? I said he wouldn't like it.'

There was no Salmon Gardens anywhere in St Stephen's Bay. Not, anyway, according to the street map Harry bought which had an index of place names on the back. The list read: '. . . Sackman Road, Saffron Road, Salmon Street, Scullion Lane . . .' Which left 'Salmon Street' as clear favourite, especially if Rose's memory hadn't been one hundred per cent.

To make certain, he called at the Planning Department, resolving this time to be more cautious in using any information they might supply. In the event all they did was to confirm the street map. They'd never heard of any Salmon Gardens either and even checked their records of neighbouring villages and hamlets without coming up with anything remotely similar.

Salmon Street it had to be then. Harry borrowed Derek's Rover and, following his map, discovered it to be a short row of pebble-dashed semis, part of a council estate on the outskirts of the town. It struck him as unpromising, not the sort of territory where you'd expect to find the origins of intimidation and murder. Even worse, there was only one side to the street, that started at number 2 and went, even numbers only, to number 34. There was no 21.

Without much hope but feeling he might as well pursue things to the bitter end, Harry tried number 20, got no answer then moved along to 22. Here he was more successful. The door was opened by a middle-aged man in carpet slippers who blinked up at Harry as though he'd just been roused from sleep.

'Sorry to trouble you,' said Harry. 'I'm trying to find a friend of mine called Nick Wyatt. I've lost his address but I'm sure it was somewhere round here.'

It wasn't a particularly clever ploy but the best he could manage given the vagueness of what Rose had been able to tell him. Nor did it produce much of a response. The man scratched his head. 'Nick who?'

'Wyatt.'

'No . . .' He turned and called over his shoulder. 'Hilda . . . ?'

Hilda shuffled into view, larger in every direction than her husband and smoking a cigarette. She smiled at Harry.

'What is it?'

'Do we know anybody called, er . . .'

'Wyatt,' completed Harry patiently. 'Nick Wyatt.'

She considered. 'There's a White lives at number four. But I think he's called Richard or something, isn't he?'

'Robert,' said her husband.

'No, this is definitely Nick Wyatt,' said Harry.

'Doesn't sound like him then.'

A young woman was passing on the other side of the road.

'Mrs Davies . . . ?' called Hilda.

'Yes, dear?'

'Do you know anybody round here called Wyatt?'

'Who, dear?' she asked, crossing to join them.

'Nick Wyatt,' said Harry.

'No. Wyatt Earp, that's all I've ever heard of.'

'Wasn't he a cowboy?' asked the man.

'The person I'm looking for is aged about twenty, quite tall, dark, good-looking,' interrupted Harry before things got completely out of hand.

Mrs Davies thought and shook her head. 'Doesn't ring a bell.'

'Me neither,' agreed Hilda.

Another neighbour was spotted and called in to help so that the group around Harry grew. So did the number of names he was offered, none of which could have been Nick. It looked as though Rose had been right after all: Salmon Gardens, not Street. Anyway, certainly not here.

Muttering thanks and apologies, Harry finally managed to extricate himself and drove away, leaving the debate still in full flow behind him. His bad luck seemed to be holding. At least, he thought, it couldn't get any worse. Then he arrived back at the arcade to find it already had.

'It's not that I don't appreciate the job you've done, Harry. . .' said Derek, fiddling with a pile of change.

'But you want me to go.'

'I just think . . . well, this business seems to have run its course and so . . .'

'OK,' said Harry resignedly. 'I'm going. Don't worry.'

'And I'm grateful. I really am.'

Harry nodded but said nothing and went to join Jill where she was waiting for him in the office at the rear of the arcade. He, of course, knew the real reason for Derek Underhill's suddenly wanting him out. And Derek knew he knew, which was why he'd been muttering and mumbling apologetically and avoiding Harry's eye. It was to keep Charlie Monroe happy. Charlie had spoken — get rid of him; he didn't want to see him around any longer — and had to be obeyed. But there wasn't much point in throwing this truth back in Derek's face. He, after all, had to live in St Stephen's Bay and with Charlie Monroe; Harry didn't. He could take the evening train to London and wash his hands of the whole business.

'What's the matter?' asked Jill, seeing his face.

'Nothing much. I've just been sacked, that's all.'

'Oh, I'm sorry.' And she looked it too, her small face creased in anxiety.

He managed a laugh. 'No. Had to happen sooner or later. Don't worry about it.'

'I haven't been much help though, have I?'

'You weren't meant to be. You were meant to be reading your books.'

'I haven't got far with them either.'

'Well, now you'll have your chance.'

He was moving to leave when she said, 'What's through there?' indicating the locked door that led back into the body of the building.

'Oh, just a load of dust and rubbish and a maze of old dressing-rooms or whatever they used to be.'

He meant to deter her, forgetting her attraction for anything musty and dusty.

'Can we go through?' she asked.

It would have been churlish to deny her that small pleasure. 'If you really want to,' he said, knowing that she certainly did. He found the key and opened the door.

'Careful,' he warned, as she went eagerly past him. 'You could break your neck in here.'

She stared around, up at the ruined ceiling with its patched skylights and the balcony running beneath it.

'Oh, it must have been glorious,' she exclaimed. 'What a shame it's been left.' He had to admire her imagination. 'If only somebody would restore it,' she went on. 'I mean it's basically still all here. It just needs cleaning and repainting.'

Or bulldozing, thought Harry. You could make a lot of improvements with a bulldozer and a steel ball on the end of a crane. But he knew better than to provoke her by suggesting it.

'Can we go back there?' she asked, looking longingly across the stage with its tantalising glimpses of hidden worlds beyond.

'It's filthy. You'll need a bath afterwards.'

'You sound like my mother,' she said tartly. 'How do I get up here?'

'I'll lift you up. But then don't move. There's a bloody great hole in the middle.'

He hoisted her on to the stage, then vaulted up beside her. He took her hand and they stepped around the edge of the hole. She peered in.

'There's scenery down there,' she said.

'Well, it can stay there.'

'Oh, and look at these. . . !' Which were the music and microphone stands, spot-lights and other rusting relics of the big band days that lay cluttering back-stage. He waited patiently as she picked at it. God knew what she expected to find. It was like the antique shops she kept dragging him into. She seemed fascinated by other people's rubbish.

'The dressing-rooms are down here,' he said, and she followed him into the narrow corridor with its walls of painted brick.

'Watch out for mice,' he said mischievously.

'Don't worry,' she said. 'They won't bite.'

They looked in each dressing-room as they came to it, though he could see she was disappointed by their bleakness. Not much here for her to exclaim over, just cracked mirrors and old, stained sinks. Only the room with the post-cards still tacked up gave her anything to enthuse about. She read them carefully.

'I wonder where these people are now. It's sad really, isn't it?' Then, getting no reply: 'Don't you think it's sad?'

'Yes,' he said. 'It's sad. Now come on, let's get out of here.'

She looked at him, surprised by the sudden note of urgency. 'What's the matter?'

'Oh, it's just . . . creepy. It's giving me the shivers. Come on.'

His admission amused her but she let him have his way and they went back together down the corridor.

'I bet this place has a ghost if only we knew,' she mused. 'Probably more than one.'

'I'd rather not find out.'

She looked at him. 'You really don't like this place, do you?'

she said, entertained by her discovery. 'I didn't know you were frightened of ghosts.'

'I've never met one.'

'Tell you what,' she said teasingly, 'let's come back tonight. See if there really are any. I bet there's a woman in a long white dress who waits every evening for the music to begin. . .'

He let her prattle on, locking the door behind them and then, when she wasn't looking, slipping the key into his pocket. He might well return tonight, yes. But he'd do so alone, not with her.

For he'd spotted something in that last dressing-room that she hadn't. A large can of paraffin. At least he'd judged it to be paraffin from the whiff he'd managed to get of it. Most definitely it hadn't been there on his previous visit. Which was why he'd had to rush her from the room before she could notice it and become curious.

In other circumstances he might have dismissed it as placed there for some innocent purpose. But too much had happened around the Winter Gardens for the innocence of anything to be taken for granted.

They left the arcade and were outside among the noise and bustle.

'So when're we going back to London?' she asked. 'Tonight?'

He had to decide quickly.

'Tomorrow,' he said.

'Whenever you like.'

'Tomorrow,' he repeated, certain now of what he would do.

The hard part had been accounting for his absence without alarming her. In the end he settled for telling half the truth and fudging the other half so that she might think he was being foolish but wouldn't suspect he'd be in danger.

'I think there might be an attempt to break into the arcade tonight. So I'm going to watch for an hour or two. Just to see if anything happens.'

Even that was enough to draw a cry of protest.

'Oh, Harry, no. You mustn't.'

'Don't worry, I'm only going to watch. Anything happens and I'll be dialling nine-nine-nine and staying well clear.'

'So why not stay clear altogether? Tell the police and let them do the watching.'

'I'd feel a bit stupid if I've got it wrong.'

'I'm going to come with you.'

'No, you're not.'

In the end it was a straight battle of wills, one that this time he was determined to win. No, he couldn't tell her what his information was, and yes, he was sure there wasn't the slightest danger. She must give him her word that she wouldn't try to follow or interfere in any way.

'I thought you said they'd sacked you,' was her final attempt to dissuade him.

'They have. That's why I want to have one last crack at it. See if I can't have the last laugh. And you know what you said about Greg's article. . . .'

'What?'

'That the only way I can stop it is by solving Nick's murder.'

'I think you're crazy.'

'I am.'

Seeing she wasn't going to shift him, she gave a groan of dismay. Then she took his hands and said, 'Just promise me — you're going to watch it from outside, and if anything happens you'll call the police. And nothing else.'

'I promise,' he lied. And left her alone in their attic room with a pile of books and a cup of cocoa.

The arcade was long closed when he arrived. He looked at his watch and saw it was just after eleven. Probably too early for anything to happen yet, with people still about, but better that than too late. He let himself in, grateful that Derek hadn't thought to ask for the return of his keys, and moved cautiously down the arcade between the banks of machines. The darkness was total. He didn't dare switch on a light but relied on memory and on his outstretched, groping hands to get him safely down the length of the arcade and into contact with the office door.

His fingers found the lock and then the key that would fit it. Into the office, and with the door closed, he was still wary about unnecessary light and so shuffled forward till a blow on his thigh told him he'd reached the desk. Opening its top drawer, he rummaged around till he found the heavy duty torch he knew was kept there. He switched it on and swept its beam around the walls. No sign yet of any intruder. But then he was still in the antechamber to this Gothic mansion.

He took out the key he'd kept from that afternoon and opened the door to the old ballroom, being careful first to switch off his torch lest its beam should go ahead of him and betray him.

He listened hard but heard nothing. Then a creak sent his pulse racing. Had it been a footstep? From where? Then another, so long as to be almost a groan. It was from above. He remained stock still till another creak convinced him it was no more than the old building settling after the heat of the day.

He risked switching on the torch again. Better that than a broken neck. He went forward in slow motion, testing each new step before allowing his weight to settle. Then up on to the stage. Around the gaping chasm at its centre, and through to the cluttered regions beyond.

The soft squealing of mice somewhere ahead gave him another small scare till he reasoned that, if they were running around, no-one else would be. There was now a chill in the air, down here in the bowels of the building. He turned up the collar of his jacket.

The can was still there, beneath the sink in the corner of the end dressing-room. He removed its cap and immediately his earlier suspicions were confirmed. Paraffin. Had this been mid-winter, it might have put him in mind of heating, a way of keeping warm; as it was, he could think only of arson, a way of finally closing the arcade for good.

He replaced the cap and explored the rest of the room. There didn't seem to be any other surprises. He settled down in a corner, the one that would put him behind the door should it open again. His watch said 11.25. He switched off the torch and placed it by his foot.

There was time enough now for doubt and second thoughts. Whoever had left the paraffin there might have done so for many reasons. His hunch told him those reasons weren't for the best but his hunches had been wrong before. And, anyway, what was there to say that whoever had deposited it there would return tonight? Why not tomorrow? Next week? Or not at all?

His only answer, which wasn't much of one, was that there'd been a quick, unbroken escalation in the threats the arcade had faced up to now. Whoever was behind this caper didn't hang about. If the paraffin signalled a new phase then it was likely to happen sooner rather than later.

And anyway — which was the real reason — he felt obliged to make a final attempt before meekly catching the train back to Victoria. And it would be a final attempt too. If nothing happened tonight then he'd happily tell Superintendent Charlton all about the paraffin and leave it to him to sit there tomorrow night, getting pins-and-needles and wishing he'd slipped a quarter-bottle of Johnny Walker into his pocket to help pass the time.

12.10. How long should he stay? Till two? His career as bouncer and barman made him something of a night-bird, accustomed to the small hours, so at least he wasn't likely to nod off. It was a bit too cold and cramped and uncomfortable for that anyway. Perhaps he'd stay till three. Three at the outside.

There was a renewed squealing of mice. Not wanting to find one exploring the inside of his trouser leg, he switched on his torch and glimpsed two small, grey bodies disappearing into the wall.

12.35. He thought of the post-cards on the wall. Switched on his torch and let its beam play on them for a moment. What life there must once have been down here, chorus-girls and musicians, perhaps the odd famous name on his or her way down, a host of new-comers hoping they were on their way up. None of them thinking they'd become old and that the building itself would decay.

Don't be so bloody morbid, he thought. Perhaps, after all, this place does have ghosts of a sort.

He thought of his own past, parts of it profligate and violent, other parts circumscribed by tight prison walls not unlike the ones of this room. Very like them in fact, save that you didn't get mice in prison — they couldn't stand it. He wondered, too, about his future, now intimately allied with Jill, so different from himself she might have come from Mars instead of just suburbia and university. Would they manage to decay together? Or would their different natures and backgrounds finally split them apart? He hoped not, but knew from hard experience that hope had little to do with it.

One o'clock. He stood up and paced the room. Did some quick exercises to keep the blood flowing. In fact, decided to make a routine of it. Every ten . . . no, fifteen minutes he'd do ten laps of the room and a minute of bends and stretches.

It was a routine he never had the chance to begin. At seven minutes past one he heard footsteps approaching. There was a glint of light under the door, then it was pushed open.

10

Harry had got to his feet at the first sound of the approach and was crouching behind the door, ready to spring. He couldn't forget that Nick had been shot. Whoever was about to enter, it didn't do to let him get the drop on you.

A beam of light came through the door and played around the walls, then a figure followed it into the room. Harry moved noiselessly forward, still hidden by the door and poised to strike, till something familiar about the silhouette made him hesitate. In that moment the figure became aware of him and swung round. Harry snapped on his own torch.

It illuminated a shocked and staring face, mouth open and eyes wide with fear. But familiar all the same. Derek Underhill.

'Bloody hell,' said Harry in surprise.

Blinded by the torch-light, Derek shouted 'Who is it? No! Don't . . . !' And raised a protective arm to his face.

'It's me,' said Harry, and shone his torch on to his own face.

'Harry . . . ? It's you, is it, Harry?'

'Yes.'

'Oh, thank Christ. Oh my God, my heart. I've got to sit down.' And he slumped to the floor.

Now it was Harry's turn to be alarmed, foreseeing himself with a dead man on his hands in circumstances that wouldn't be easy to explain. 'Take it easy,' he muttered. 'You'll be OK.' Though for a while he doubted it. Derek seemed to be losing consciousness, was panting for breath. Harry looked round for some water but the old taps wouldn't turn. Then, slowly, Derek's gasps became less desperate and his head came up from between his knees.

'You're all right?' asked Harry, greatly relieved.

'Will be . . . yes.'

'Just take it easy.'

'I will. Bit of a shock, that's all. Be all right in a minute.'

He shook his head as though to clear it and then struggled to hoist himself back on to his feet. Harry bent to assist, taking his weight. It also gave him the opportunity to make sure Derek didn't have a gun tucked away somewhere. He did a quick, surreptitious check but could feel nothing, either under the jacket or in the pockets, as he solicitously dusted him down.

The fact that it was Derek Underhill who'd come through the door, and not some anonymous thug, left Harry wondering how best to proceed. He'd taken it for granted that whoever entered would be the perpetrator of the arcade's troubles and Nick's murderer. Did finding that it was the arcade's owner, the man who'd employed him to put a stop to those troubles, change all that?

'Christ, you gave me a shock,' said Derek. 'I can do without too many of them, I can tell you.'

'It was a bit of a surprise for me as well,' said Harry. He placed his own torch so that it pointed into the cracked mirror and spread its light upon the two of them.

'What're you doing here anyway?' asked Derek.

'Waiting to see who else might turn up. What're you?'

'Me? Oh, tour of the premises. Just keeping an eye on my valuable property, you know how it is.'

'At this time of night?'

'I was passing anyway. On my way home, you know. And then I remembered it was old Reg locking up tonight. And, well, he's not the most reliable, is he?'

It was all a touch too eager. It should have been Harry having to explain himself to Derek, not vice versa.

'But what made you come back here?'

'Ah well, like I say, I was checking the arcade and then I thought I heard somebody. Must have been you, mustn't it?'

At which Harry's lingering doubts dispersed: he didn't believe a word of it. Any slight noise he might have made couldn't possibly have carried back and through into the shell of the arcade. Derek was lying. Had to be.

'So you came down to investigate.'

'I did, yes.'

'You're a braver man than I am.'

'How d'you mean?'

'Well, the middle of the night. Black as the ace of spades. You think you hear an intruder and so you come to have a look. You're lucky it was only me.'

'Well, not an intruder exactly, no. I thought it was more likely a cat or . . . well, a cat, probably.'

'You got any matches?'

'What?'

'Matches. Have you got any?'

Derek's hand went to his pocket, then stopped.

'Never mind what I've got or haven't got,' he said, beginning to bluster. 'I don't see why I'm having to answer to you about what I'm doing here. It's my property.'

'Of course it is,' agreed Harry calmly.

'Yes, right. So what about you? What're you doing here? I told you this afternoon I didn't want you on the job any more.'

For an answer Harry stepped to the can of paraffin and kicked it with the toe of his shoe.

'I'm minding this.'

'Oh yes, and what's that when it's at home?'

'Paraffin.'

There was a silence. It's not that he's surprised, thought Harry. It's that he's trying to work out just what his reaction would be had he really known nothing about it.

'Paraffin, eh?'

'Yes.'

'Well, and who's put that there?'

'If I knew that I wouldn't have had to sit here tonight,' said Harry. 'As it was, all I could do was wait to see who turned up to claim it.'

'Oh.'

'And lo and behold . . . turns out to be you.'

'I hope you're not implying anything by that?'

'No.'

'I hope you're not implying I'm intending to set fire to my own premises.'

'No.'

'Good.'

'Looks like somebody's intending to, though.'

'You think so?'

'Why else should they want to hide a gallon of paraffin back here?'

Derek thought about it. Or, anyway, appeared to. 'It could have been here for some time. Years perhaps.'

'No, it couldn't. It wasn't here when I had a wander round three days ago.'

'Oh.' Then reluctantly: 'Oh well, looks like you're right then. Looks like chummy's up to his tricks again.'

'And you still don't have any idea just who chummy might be?'

'Me? Not a clue, no. I only wish I did.' He gestured towards the can of paraffin. 'Whoever it is though, I think we'd be wise to get rid of this stuff, don't you?' And he stepped towards it.

'No,' said Harry sharply. Derek stopped and looked at him. 'Don't touch it.'

To make sure he didn't, he placed himself between Derek and the can. Then explained: 'There'll be finger-prints on it. It'll give the police something to go on at last.'

'Oh yes. Of course there will, yes,' said Derek. He didn't sound over-enthusiastic. 'I, er, I wasn't thinking.'

Harry wished he could see him better. The fractured torch-light threw shadows and left areas of darkness. Faces were either in gloomy outline or thrown into lurid relief. Either way, it was difficult to read much from the other man's expression.

'Whoever's prints are on there is the bastard that shot Nick,' said Harry, seeking to maintain the pressure. 'So the last thing we want to do is spoil 'em. In fact, what I suggest is that we leave it right where it is and go and use your phone.'

'Yes,' agreed Derek, but didn't move. His eyes went to the can again, then back to Harry. As if he were having to choose between them.

'Once they've got that to go on, they'll soon have everything wrapped up,' said Harry, to encourage him into the right decision. 'Finger-prints. Forensic evidence. They'll be in their element.'

Another pause. Then Derek gave a small groan and shook his head.

'What?' said Harry.

'No. Please, Harry, we don't have to drag the police in, do we?'

He was close to submission. Just don't be too keen, Harry warned himself. Wind him in nice and slowly. He could still turn tail, refuse to say another word and charge Harry with trespass; then where would they be?

'It's up to you,' said Harry slowly. 'I mean I'm no great friend of the police.'

Derek was quick to bite. 'Right. Course you're not. That's why I brought you in. Then we could sort it all out without 'em.'

'Trouble is, Derek, there's still too much I don't understand.'

'You don't?'

'No.'

'Well . . . like what?'

'Like what you're doing here tonight.'

'I told you—'

'Oh, I know what you told me. But let's be honest, it's not every night you come back here chasing cats, is it?'

Derek hesitated, licked his lips nervously, then said, 'No. No, it isn't.'

'Then why don't you tell me the truth?'

There was a moment when it might have gone either way and he might have reverted to his earlier blustering; then he said, 'You know anyway.'

Harry's heart leapt. 'I'd still like you to tell me. Just to be sure.'

'It's me,' he said simply. Then, when Harry waited for more, added, 'Everything that's been happening. It's all been me.'

'And tonight?'

'I was going to make a bonfire out of this place. I brought the paraffin this morning. I didn't think it'd look as suspicious as it would at night.' Then he grabbed Harry's arm and said urgently, 'But I didn't have nothing to do with what happened to Nick. I swear to God I had nothing to do with that, Harry.'

'You didn't . . . ?'

'I didn't, no. Now you've got to believe that, Harry. You've got to.'

Harry wondered. Now he'd got the confession he'd been seeking, was it a confession at all? Or was this no more than a sordid bargain he was being offered — forget the major crime and I'll put my name to the rest? Because he could stuff that. He wasn't going to be party to that.

'I don't know what to believe, do I? Not till I'm told a hell of a sight more about what's going on.'

Derek nodded. 'But no police?'

Harry shrugged. 'Depends.'

'On what?'

'On what you have to tell me.'

'I'll tell you everything. No choice, have I?'

'Not a lot.'

'I'll tell you everything you want to know, Harry. I swear. Just so long as we can leave the police out of it.'

For a moment the light was right. Harry saw the desperation on Derek's face and knew that, whatever the truth was, he was about to hear it.

'All right. Tell me then.'

'Can we go back to the office? Only I wouldn't half mind a drink.'

'I don't see why not,' said Harry, who wasn't too fond of their present accommodation himself.

'And can we bring that?' Meaning the can of paraffin in the corner. Seeing Harry's hesitation, he gave a small laugh. 'Don't worry, I'm not trying anything clever. Just don't want it left back here, that's all. Might be a fire-risk.'

If it was a joke, Harry wasn't in any mood for it. But nor could he see that it really mattered whether the can stayed or went with them. All his talk about finger-prints had been as much a matter of bluff as anything else, since all he knew for certain was that his own were liberally pasted around the can. 'I'll bring it,' he said. And, torch in one hand, paraffin can in the other, he motioned to Derek to lead off.

They went down the corridor without speaking and in single file, retracing together the route they'd separately followed earlier. Over the stage and across the ballroom floor. It was a relief to reach the office and be able to switch on its lights.

'What are you doing?' asked Harry, as Derek opened a filing-cabinet.

Derek raised his hands in a gesture of innocence. 'A drink.'

'Let me see.'

And he looked carefully, still on his guard, still mindful of the gun that had accounted for Nick and that presumably still existed somewhere. But it wasn't in the filing-cabinet that housed a bottle of Scotch and two glasses.

'OK now?' asked Derek and, at Harry's nod, retrieved the bottle and glasses. He poured two generous measures. 'Cheers,' he said, and downed half of his. Then clutched at his stomach and winced with pain.

'Still suffering?' said Harry.

'Too true I am. And suffering's the word for it, believe me, Harry boy. Suffering with my guts. Suffering with this place.'

He finished the drink in another gulp and poured himself some more.

'So,' said Harry. 'Tell me.'

'Where is it you want me to start?'

Harry, who wasn't sure, decided to start with the can of paraffin and work backwards.

'You put that paraffin there?'

'Yes.'

'With the intention of coming back tonight and burning down the entire building.'

'Yes.'

'Why?'

'Insurance.'

Harry took a drink to give himself time to consider that. As a motive it was straightforward and hardly original. But how well did it fit Derek Underhill, a man who owned a lucrative business and drove a 3·5 litre Rover? Could it really be worth the risk of losing everything in return for a single cheque from what had to be a highly suspicious insurance company?

'As simple as that?'

'Yes.'

'Insurance.'

'Yes.'

'But surely . . .' Harry shook his head, not yet convinced. 'You can't need money that badly . . . ?'

'Oh, can I not? Well, let me tell you something, Harry. I am in debt. I'm up to my neck in debt.'

'Who to?'

Derek smiled.

It was a reaction that surprised Harry, who could only suppose it was from relief at knowing he'd been rumbled and could at last afford the luxury of confession. It was a relief he'd experienced himself and could have understood.

But no, it wasn't that. When he spoke again, Harry saw immediately the reason for his wry amusement.

'Casinos,' he said.

'Casinos . . . ?' echoed Harry.

Derek nodded. 'One in Brighton, one up in the Smoke. Of course I've lost money in others as well, but they're the main two.

And I owe them a lot of money and they want paying.'

Harry regarded him, no longer doubting the truth of what he was hearing.

'I see. I'd never have taken you for a gambler.'

'Oh, I'm a gambler all right. And I'm a loser as well.'

'They all are, aren't they? Sooner or later.'

Derek nodded and reached for some more of the whisky. 'Quite right, Harry. As you so wisely observe, we all are. Sooner or later we all are.'

'But I'd have thought . . . well, with the arcade and everything, you must know it's a mug's game if anybody does.'

'Course I do, yes. Doesn't stop me being a mug though, does it?'

No, thought Harry, who'd witnessed all varieties of mugs, hooked on to everything from drugs to black suspenders. And gambling perhaps most of all. Horses, cards, dice, dogs . . . if it moved, bet on it.

'Is that why you had the idea of turning this place into a casino?'

'I suppose so, yes.'

It was nice to think he hadn't been too far off the mark then. Casinos were, after all, at the root of this little mystery, though not quite in the way Harry had guessed.

'If you can't beat 'em, join 'em,' said Derek. 'Only they wouldn't let me do that so . . . well, things went from bad to worse. I've lost thousands, Harry. You wouldn't believe. Thousands. Can't believe it myself.' He was becoming maudlin with the drink.

'But this business must be worth a fair amount. Why not just sell it?'

Derek was already shaking his head. 'Who wants it? Oh, the arcade, yes. They'd have that all right. But you take the arcade and you have to take this monstrosity of a building as well. And nobody in their right mind is going to do that, I can promise you.'

'No?'

'It's like a mill-stone. A bloody great mill-stone round my neck is what this place is and has been for years. It costs me money. Rates, insurance, you name it. It costs me money and I get nothing in return. I can't afford to rebuild it. And I can't knock it down 'cause it's what they call a listed building. I've no choice, Harry. I've been driven to this. I've had no bloody choice.'

It was all becoming clear. The super-glue, the undertakers and the rest of it . . . it was all becoming crystal clear.

'So all the bother you were having . . .'

'Yes,' said Derek.

'You planned all that?'

'All me, yes. I set it all up.' At least he had the grace to look shame-faced as he admitted, 'See, I wanted 'em thinking there was somebody who'd got it in for me. Then when this place burnt down . . .'

He left it unsaid. Nor did it need saying. Once the place had burnt down, the history of sabotage would have been discovered, deflecting any suspicions the police or insurance company might harbour regarding Derek Underhill's role in the scheme of things. It would have gone down as the final act of the unknown, unseen saboteur. Derek would have collected his insurance, property companies would have been falling over themselves to develop the prime site and everybody would have been laughing but for the local Civic Trust who would have bemoaned the loss to the town's architectural heritage.

It would have also gone down on record as another failure for Harry Sommers, private detective. The man who'd supposedly been called in to get to the source of the trouble, but who, in reality, had been called in to provide a cast-iron alibi for arsonist Derek. How would anyone ever have dared to question his innocence after he'd gone to the length, and expense, of employing a private detective?

As if he could read Harry's thoughts, Derek said, 'And I'm sorry about, er, you know, about getting you involved.'

'You were having me for a fool,' said Harry, as the full truth sunk in.

'No, Harry—'

'Yes!' And he banged his fist on the table in a sudden fit of anger and frustration that sent the remaining whisky jumping from his glass.

He thought of how he'd worried about the case, how he'd fought alongside Nick against the four yobboes, how he'd been viewed by the police as a murder suspect. He'd a right to be annoyed. He'd a right to be bloody furious. To douse Derek Underhill with his own paraffin and march him down to the police-station at the point of a loaded cigarette-lighter.

'I'm sorry, Harry,' repeated Derek. 'And listen, I didn't have anything to do with what happened to Nick. That was terrible was that. That wasn't anything to do with me.'

'And I'm supposed to believe that, am I?'

'You've got to believe it, Harry, 'cause it's the truth. I swear on my mother's grave it's the truth.'

You owe this man nothing, Harry reminded himself, not even a fair hearing. And yet it was difficult to disbelieve him, much as he might strive to.

'How do I know Nick didn't find out what was going on?'

'He didn't. He'd have said something to you if he had.'

'Not necessarily. He might have tried blackmailing you. Which was why you decided to shoot him.'

'No, Harry, I swear. There was nothing like that.'

'Prove it.'

'Well, I haven't got a gun, have I? How would I shoot him? I've never done anything like that in my life.'

'So who did?'

'I don't know. Honest to God, I don't.'

Harry got to his feet and paced the office. Derek watched him, then poured some more whisky into his glass.

'I'm glad you stopped me. Stopped me doing what I was going to. You can think what you like about me but I'll always be grateful to you. I must have been mad. I don't know what came over me.'

'Nothing came over you,' said Harry bitterly. 'You had it all nicely planned. If you'd have had your way this place would've been an inferno by now.'

'I'm still grateful,' said Derek. 'Don't think I'm not.'

'Grateful 'cause you think you're getting away with it.'

'I'm not getting away with anything, Harry. I'm going to have to sell my house, everything. Even try and get what I can for this place. No, I'm finished. Doesn't matter what you do, I'm finished anyway.'

As well you deserve to be, thought Harry. Though it still didn't help him see his way ahead. Should he play it by the book and turn Derek Underhill over to the police? He might not have got round to arson but there were doubtless other charges which could be brought against him.

But then how would his own role appear, exposed as it would have to be in court and relayed from there by Greg and his colleagues for all to enjoy? At best he'd feature as the easily duped private eye. At worst there'd be reference to his own criminal past and speculation that he'd been in league with Derek Underhill, providing the alibi in exchange for a share in the insurance money. Hobson's choice.

'Have a drink, Harry,' said Derek hopefully. 'Sit down and have a drink.'

In the end he did. Just to make it clear that it didn't make them friends, he told Derek what he thought of him — that he was a dishonest, conniving trickster who richly deserved whatever financial hell the casinos were going to put him through. Derek nodded and agreed. He was all of these things. And he'd remain eternally grateful to Harry for saving him from himself.

Though there was one point on which he still insisted. 'But you believe me about Nick, don't you, Harry? I had nothing to do with that. You believe that, don't you?'

Harry sighed and finally, reluctantly, said that yes, he believed him. He didn't want to, but there was something about the man that forced him to admit it. He might have been the least admirable of all St Stephen's Bay's citizens but he would have struck no-one, either on first or further acquaintance, as a murderer.

Harry found himself yawning.

'Come on,' he said, standing. 'I want to get some sleep if you don't.'

'Sleep?' said Derek. 'I won't be sleeping, not tonight. Don't know when I'll ever sleep again, and that's the truth.'

They came out of the arcade, Derek bringing with him his can of paraffin. It was a clear night, though cooler than of late with a thin breeze rising off the sea.

A policeman came strolling past and eyed them curiously.

'Good night, officer,' said Derek.

'Good night,' said the officer, and went on his way.

It was a small encounter but one that left Harry feeling like an accomplice. Certainly if he'd ever had any intention of reporting Derek, it was too late now.

'Good night then, Harry,' said Derek, holding out a hand.

Harry took it in a brief handshake. 'Good night.'

'Oh, and, needless to say, as soon as you care to let me have your bill . . .'

'You'll get it,' said Harry, cutting him short for fear there'd be the hint of a generous bonus for his cooperation in turning a blind eye to Derek's misdemeanours. It was bad enough feeling he'd been compromised without having that feeling confirmed by an offer of money.

They parted, with more expressions of gratitude from Derek. Harry walked along the promenade, which was now all but deserted. It had been an eventful night, at the end of which he now understood a good deal more than he had at the beginning. The only thing he understood even less about was Nick's murder.

He arrived back at Floribunda and let himself in. The house was silent, its inmates sleeping peacefully. Harry took off his shoes in the hallway and tiptoed up the flights of stairs to the room at the top. The light was still on, revealing how Jill had fallen asleep, her book still held in one hand. He gently removed it, undressed, and climbed into bed beside her.

He was congratulating himself on having managed it without disturbing her when she said sleepily, 'Did anything happen?'

'No,' he said. 'Go back to sleep.'

'I'm glad.' And then, obediently, she rolled over and resumed her steady breathing.

For Harry it wasn't so easy. He lay awake, unable to clear his head of all that had happened, still unsure of whether he'd acted for the best. In the end he had to recognise that what was done was done. His decision not to report Derek and to accept his claims of innocence regarding Nick's murder would stand for eternity.

Looking on the positive side — and being somewhat surprised to find there was one — he'd accomplished the task for which he'd been hired. He'd discovered who was behind the harassment of the arcade and he'd put a stop to it. However Derek Underhill solved his financial problems, it wouldn't be by arson.

As for Nick's murder . . . even here he'd made progress of a sort. He now knew it wasn't connected with anything else that had happened at the Winter Gardens. The police, who weren't yet aware of this, were still looking in the wrong place and for the wrong thing.

He felt as if he were coming upon the murder for the very first time, unencumbered by misleading assumptions. It opened up a host of new possibilities. Regarding, for one thing, the whereabouts of the elusive number 21 Salmon Gardens. It meant, too, thinking about Nick's life beyond the arcade and into what dubious acquaintance he might have fallen.

'Tomorrow,' muttered Harry to himself, as he finally drifted into a fitful sleep. It was a promise of things he would do.

11

He was still yawning at breakfast the next morning, prompting Jill to ask, 'What time did you get back last night?'

'Oh, not late,' he said evasively.

'Two-thirty,' she said, then smiled at his surprise. 'I looked at my watch when I heard you come in.'

'They why ask?'

'Just thought I'd see how honest you were.'

'Well, now you know I'm not.'

'You said that nothing had happened. Were you being honest about that?'

'More or less. Nothing happened as I expected it to.' She looked at him, spoon suspended above her cornflakes, and clearly waiting for more. 'Derek Underhill turned up.'

'The man who owns the place . . . ?'

'Yes.'

'Oh, I see. So you spent the rest of the night drinking together?'

'Sort of.'

Mary brought their eggs and bacon, gave Harry a sidelong glance and hurried away. Ever since the murder, her attitude towards him had been a mix of curiosity and horror.

'These eggs get worse every day,' said Jill, inspecting her plate. 'Thank God this is the last.'

'Well, not quite,' said Harry.

'Why? We're leaving today, aren't we?'

'Tomorrow.'

She looked at him in surprise. 'Tomorrow?'

'You don't mind, do you?'

It wasn't so much that she minded as that she couldn't understand it. 'But we were going to go yesterday and then you wanted to hang on for last night. I thought you said you were sacked? That your services are no longer required and all that?'

'Yes, I was. And no, they weren't. But then last night . . . well, I got talking to Derek . . .'

He was lost for an explanation and so was grateful when she supplied her own.

'Oh, I see . . . You had a drink together and now you're big buddies again.'

'Something like that.'

If that's what she chose to believe then he wasn't going to enlighten her. There might be a time for the truth but it wouldn't be till this was all over.

'I don't mind if *you* want to go back today,' he said. 'Then I'll join you tomorrow.'

Part of him said it would be better that way. He didn't know what the next twenty-four hours might produce — probably nothing — but at least, without her to consider, he'd be able to concentrate his energies on the single and all-important task of tracing Nick's killer.

She seemed in two minds herself and took a moment to answer.

'Oh, I might as well stay. Keep you company. That's if you're sure it's only going to be till tomorrow. I don't want to find we're still here at Christmas.'

'We'll go tomorrow,' he promised. 'Do you mind if I make a quick phone-call?'

'Course not.'

'I'll be back in a minute.'

He threaded his way out between the tables. Conversation was about the weather. Those who'd ventured outdoors before breakfast had returned with tales of lower temperatures and overcast skies.

Harry reached the pay-phone in the hallway, told the operator he wanted to make a reverse charge call and asked for the agency's number.

The first thing Yvonne said was, 'This must be costing a fortune.'

'Then make sure we stick it on the bill.'

'Just so long as we can get him to pay it.'

'Oh, I don't think you need worry about that. He'll pay all right.'

'Have there been any new developments then?'

'Yes. Very unexpected they were too. Not all the villains are up there in London, I can tell you.'

'You've found out who shot that young man.'

''Fraid not. In fact, I was hoping you might be able to help me there.'

'What do you want?'

'Have you got an *A to Z*?'

'I will have in a minute.' He waited as she left the phone to collect it. 'Yes?'

'Can you look up Salmon Gardens?'

He heard the rustling of pages and kept his fingers crossed. If he drew a blank here then he didn't know where to turn. It was the events of last night that had freed him from his assumption that Salmon Gardens had to be local. After that, it had the distinctive ring of a London address.

'Yes?' said Yvonne.

'There is one?'

'Salmon Gardens SW7. Oh yes, there is one all right.'

Harry gave a sigh of relief. It might, he knew, still be the wrong Salmon Gardens, or, even if it were the right one, turn out to be irrelevant to Nick's sad fate. For the time being, though, it felt like a break, the first he'd had on the case and a long time coming. Should he now take a train to London himself or could Yvonne be entrusted with the task of checking out the inhabitants of number 21?

'I need to know who lives at an address there,' he said, waiting for her response.

'I see. Right. I'll find out then, shall I?'

That was positive enough. She was clearly relishing her new-found responsibilities and welcomed the prospect of more.

'Do you think you can?'

'I don't see why not.'

Nor did he. 'It's number twenty-one,' he said. 'Oh, and it's urgent. I need to know today.'

'Tell me where I can ring you and I'll see what I can do.'

He gave her the number of the arcade and said he'd be there all morning. She promised to be in touch and rang off.

He went back into the dining-room. Mary, who was collecting plates, shied away at his approach and dropped a knife on the carpet. Perhaps he should have gone himself, he thought, struck by sudden misgivings. Though Yvonne had sounded confident enough. He must have faith in her. At least she knew nothing about the case and so had no preconceptions about what she might be walking into. Should he have warned her? Might she be in any danger? If so, her own real innocence was probably her best protection.

He sat down again and set about the congealing egg and bacon. Jill had abandoned hers and was in the process of dropping a sweetener from its dispenser on to her palm and from there into her coffee.

'So, shall I make myself scarce?' she asked. 'Go and find a place in the sun while you work in your mysterious ways?'

He gave her a grateful smile. 'Well, I'm going to be at the arcade all morning. I don't think you'd find it much fun.'

'I'm sure I wouldn't,' she said with a shudder.

'I'll see you at lunchtime then, shall I?'

Their arrangements made, they climbed the thirty-nine steps that took them to their room, a number Jill had already commented on as being sinister and significant and, anyway, far too many for comfort. Once there, they cleaned their teeth, checked they had everything necessary for the day ahead — money, books, notepads, pens, keys, combs — and then descended together. The penalty for forgetting anything — another climb up the thirty-nine steps — was a powerful aide-mémoire and meant they never did.

'Where are you thinking of going?' he asked as they strolled down to the promenade.

'I'm not sure,' she said, looking up at the gathering clouds. 'Perhaps somewhere with a roof on.'

They parted with a chaste kiss, and Harry headed for the arcade. He found an unexpected relief in seeing the ornate façade still intact. What would have been the scene had Derek Underhill not been stopped? A pall of smoke, piles of rubble . . . fire-engines, roads closed . . . all the trappings of disaster. Harry had done St Stephen's Bay quite a service, come to think of it. A pity it had to remain unrecognised.

He went into the arcade and found Reg in the change booth.

'Boss is in the back if you want him,' he said.

'No rush,' said Harry. 'How're you these days?'

Reg grimaced and shook his head. 'I can't get over what happened to Nick. And then nobody knows what's going to happen next, do they? I mean is any of us safe any more?'

'Oh, I think so,' said Harry.

'I just wish they'd catch whoever did it. I shan't rest happy till they do.'

A couple of children came wanting change. Reg dealt it out with a practised hand. Harry waited until they'd moved away before saying, with what he hoped was the casual air of one who'd just thought of the idea, 'Suppose that Nick's murder had nothing to do with the arcade?'

Reg looked at him. 'How d'you work that one out?'

'I'm just saying "suppose". I mean we don't know, do we?'

'I'd have thought it was bloody obvious,' said Reg.

Harry sighed and tried again. 'Just imagine though — just for the sake of argument — that whoever killed him wasn't the person behind the other stuff, then can you think of anything else Nick was involved in that might have got him bumped off?'

Reg sniffed disdainfully and shook his head.

141

'Just try and remember,' urged Harry. 'Anything he might have said. Anybody who might have come here to see him.'

Reg's head-shaking suddenly stopped. 'I'll tell you what I have just remembered.'

'What?' asked Harry hopefully.

'What we talked about that night. Regarding the plans to turn this place into a casino. . . . Now that's what you ought to be looking into.'

'I already have,' said Harry, disappointed. 'And so have the police. It was all over-and-above-board. Certainly got nothing to do with what happened to Nick.'

It was Reg's turn to be disappointed. 'Oh. Oh well, it's no use asking me then.'

It probably wasn't, thought Harry. More punters arrived, eager to change their money into the coins of this particular realm. Harry took the opportunity to slip away. It'd been a forlorn hope, anyway, asking Reg to remember beyond his last boozing session.

The curtains that shut off Rose's private, gypsy world were pulled back, wide and inviting, which suggested that she hadn't anyone with her. Harry stuck his head in cautiously — he didn't want to intrude on anyone's future — but no, Rose was there alone, reading the morning paper which she'd propped up against her crystal ball.

'Got a minute?' he asked.

'Course I have, dear. Come in. Sit yourself down and I'll make us a cup of tea, shall I?'

'I don't want to interfere with business.'

'Oh, don't worry about that. I don't get much in the mornings anyway. They generally only come after they've had a drink or two to give 'em courage. You wouldn't believe how terrified some of 'em are. I try and read their palms and I can't because they're shaking like a jelly.'

During which she'd switched on an electric kettle and produced two cups and two saucers out of a cupboard.

'I think I'd be scared about hearing my future,' said Harry.

'Well, you'd have no cause to, not from me. I never tell anybody anything bad, even if I feel it might be there. I think it'd be wrong to do a thing like that.'

'Wrong?' he queried, struck by the observation.

'Well, they come to me for a bit of hope, don't they? They want to be told things are going to get better, not worse. Because, quite honestly, most of the people who come to see me have enough troubles as it is. So the best I can do is give 'em what they're paying me for. A bit of hope and encouragement to keep 'em going for a while longer. Now, milk and sugar is it?'

Harry said yes and was given his cup. Rose collected her own and joined him at the table.

'Have they found out anything about Nick yet, do you know?' she asked.

'If they have then nobody's told me about it.'

'What about that address I gave you — Salmon Gardens?'

'All I know for sure is that it's not local. There's no Salmon Gardens in St Stephen's Bay or anywhere near.' No need to mention yet the possibility of it having turned up in London.

'Oh dear.'

'I was wondering if perhaps we've been looking for the wrong thing all along,' said Harry. 'I mean, suppose that Nick's murder had nothing to do with the other troubles . . . ?'

She was quicker on the uptake than Reg and more willing to entertain the hypothesis.

'Then it might have been for some other reason altogether?'

'It's possible,' said Harry, knowing it was a great deal more than that. It was a cast-iron certainty, though he couldn't announce it as such without exposing Derek Underhill's role in all that had happened. 'Did Nick ever mention being in any trouble?'

'Well, what sort of trouble?'

'I don't know. Money, women, anything . . . ?'

She considered. 'Not that might have led to anything as dreadful as that,' she said finally. 'He might sometimes have been short of money, yes. But he knew he could always come to me and I'd lend him whatever he needed.'

'And he paid you back?'

'Oh yes. As soon as Derek gave him his wage he'd be in here to pay what he owed.'

'Did anybody ever come to the arcade asking for him?'

'Once or twice, yes.' She gave a little smile. 'Young girls mostly. He'd sometimes hide from them and they'd look so upset. I used to say to him — you'll get your just deserts one day, and then don't come crying on my shoulder.'

'Just deserts . . . ?' queried Harry, not sure what form of retribution she had in mind.

'All I meant was that one day he'd fall for a young lady who'd treat him like he'd treated so many others.' Then she added, 'Not that many would, mind. He had a way about him that few could resist.' Which led her to a further thought: 'Terrible to think of all that he's lost, isn't it? A young man like that with all his life in front of him.'

Harry let a respectful few seconds elapse before gently prompting her: 'Did he ever have any serious trouble with any of these girls?'

'Not really, no. Most of them were only here for the week, you see. They'd usually turn up here on their last day to say goodbye to him.'

'No fathers or boyfriends threatening to knock his head off?'

'Not that I ever heard of.'

Harry cast around for another angle and recalled the question he'd had put to him by Superintendent Charlton.

'He never had anything to do with drugs, did he?'

Rose pulled a face. 'Oh no, I'm sure he didn't. Never.'

It was an expression of blind faith as much as anything, but one Harry felt inclined to go along with. From what he'd seen of him and heard about him, Nick Wyatt had had too much going for him to have need of that particular brand of poison.

'I wish I could be more help,' said Rose forlornly. 'I do really.'

But this was a consultation beyond her usual formula. The past was proving harder to decipher than the future, and she sought in vain for those words of hope and encouragement with which she rewarded most of her clients.

Salmon Gardens was a six-storey block of flats, built in the thirties, with views that had long since been curtailed by other, taller buildings. However, it retained before it a modest square of garden for the use of residents only and was near the tube and shops. Buying one of its two-bed, one recep-with-balcony flats would cost a pretty penny, thought Yvonne as she stood before it. She put her *A to Z* away in her bag and addressed herself to her task.

There were two entrances to Salmon Gardens, one reasonably plush, with worn carpets, an unlit chandelier and a porter sitting smoking behind a desk, the other smaller, starkly functional and, so far as Yvonne could see, unsupervised. It looked the better bet of the two. She went up the steps and entered, assuming an eager and slightly bewildered expression for the benefit of anyone who might be observing her. For once in her life she felt her appearance to be in her favour; wonderful indeed to feel that being not a little overweight and plain in looks could at last be counted an asset.

In the event, there seemed to be no-one around. All that faced her was an old-fashioned lift of black ironwork and, by the side of it, a notice showing which flats were on which floors. 1 to 16 were on the ground floor. 17 to 33 were on the first. She pulled open the heavy lift doors and stepped inside.

The first floor corridor was carpeted and dimly lit. 17 was the number of the first door she came to. 21 was the fifth. It had a flush, green surface with a spy-hole set in the middle and a letter-box at waist height. Beside the door-knob were two keyholes and a bell-push. No name, though, which was a pity since finding one would have made everything a great deal easier. Nothing daunted, she squared her shoulders, rehearsed her opening lines in her head and pressed the bell.

It turned out to be more buzzer than bell, harsh and insistent, so that she hesitated to press it again, even when no-one seemed to be responding. Then, suddenly, the light coming through the spy-hole was blocked off and she realised she was being observed. Her heart went a little faster: she wasn't accustomed to these games of deception and found them rather exciting.

The door opened, though not far. A woman's head and shoulder and foot appeared, all of which seemed quite young. Her hair was covered by a scarf and, so far as Yvonne could judge, she seemed to be fashionably and expensively dressed.

'Yes?' It was more a challenge than a welcome.

'Good news for you, Mrs Banerjee.'

'Pardon?'

'Good news. From the makers of the nation's favourite toilet soap.' Then after a carefully timed pause: 'You are Mrs Banerjee, aren't you?'

'No.'

Thank God for that, thought Yvonne, while managing a small pantomime of surprise and dismay.

'Oh dear, I hope there hasn't been some mistake. You wouldn't believe the things that've happened since we got computerised. . .' And she fiddled in her bag, as though in the hope of finding there the document that would explain it all.

The woman in the scarf gave a sigh of impatience.

'And your name isn't Banerjee?' repeated Yvonne.

'No.'

'It's not something that sounds like Banerjee, is it?'

'No.'

She obviously wasn't one for taking a hint, forcing Yvonne to the direct question: 'What is your name please?'

'Look, I really think you've got the wrong address. And, even if you haven't, I'm sure I'm not interested in your soap company or whatever it is. Thank you.'

And she closed the door. Damn, thought Yvonne, who felt she'd carried things off quite well and deserved better. On the other side of the door the safety-chain was slid into place and an eye applied to the spy-hole. Yvonne went off down the corridor in the opposite direction to the one from which she'd approached.

Here she found a more automated lift, whose doors opened at the touch of a button. She stepped inside and pressed another button that closed them and took her down to the ground floor. It was a journey of no more than a few seconds, yet it was time enough for her to realise that there'd been something distinctly odd about the woman-who-wasn't-Mrs-Banerjee. She also had time to realise what it was, before the lift doors re-opened to reveal the lobby she'd glimpsed from the street, with the porter behind his desk.

She came out of the lift and headed for the door, bestowing a smile and a cheery 'Hello' to the porter, who nodded and said, 'Morning.' She reached out to open the glass door that led to the street, then, hoping the porter's eyes were still on her, stopped abruptly, shook her head in dismay and turned as if to retrace her steps.

He was indeed watching her. The performance hadn't been wasted.

'How silly can you get. . . !' she exclaimed.

'Forgotten something?' he asked sympathetically.

Yvonne advanced to the desk, lowering her voice confidentially. 'I've only forgotten the lady's name, haven't I? We're doing the flowers for her party. I've got the order, got the address . . . but no name. She will think I'm stupid, won't she?'

'One of the flats here?' said the porter.

'Yes,' said Yvonne hopefully. 'Number twenty-one. You couldn't just tell me her name, could you? I'd be so grateful.'

'Well, we're not supposed to . . .'

'Oh, I wouldn't say I'd got it from you.'

He smiled. 'I think we might stretch a point. You aren't planning a burglary or anything, are you?'

Yvonne giggled disarmingly. The porter reached into the top drawer of his desk and pulled out a long card, listing names and numbers. 'Number twenty-one . . . ?' he said, and ran his finger down until he found the name.

Harry left Rose, thanking her for the tea, and went to seek out Derek Underhill in the office at the rear of the arcade. It wasn't that he particularly wanted to see him or expected to learn much from him. More a matter of re-establishing lines of communication after what had happened last night.

Derek was at the table, which was covered in papers. He looked up as Harry entered, said an abrupt hello, and then looked down again.

Harry closed the door. 'I'm staying till tomorrow,' he said.

'Right, fine.' It was a show of indifference that was as irritating as it was unconvincing.

'I won't be going to the police. But, of course, if I ever hear of this place going up in flames then I might have a change of mind.'

Derek gave up the pretence of being absorbed in his work and stared at him. 'You won't hear about it,' he said stiffly. 'It won't happen. I might be a fool but . . .' And a gesture that meant there were limits even to his foolishness.

He looked unwell, thought Harry, seeing his strained features. Perhaps he'd been awake all night, fearing Harry would shop him, or fearing his creditors. In fact, with more to fear than any of them, save whoever pulled the trigger on Nick.

Softening his tone, Harry said, 'I've been thinking about the murder.'

'So have I,' said Derek quickly.

'Yes?'

'And when it happened I was at home with the missus. That's what I told the police and that's the truth. You can ask her if you like.'

Harry shook his head. 'I believe you.'

'You do?'

He nodded. 'I believed you last night.'

Which seemed some small relief, even if all it did was remind him of what other misfortunes he had to face.

'Christ, Harry, I'm in it up to here. I'm going to have to sell every last bleeding thing I can lay my hands on. And I don't know how to break it to the wife. It's been her pride and joy has that house, but it's going to have to go.' Harry shook his head, offering sympathy but no advice. 'And the car. Why don't you make me an offer for it, eh? Motor back to London in style.'

'No, thanks.'

'It's in good nick. Eighteen months old. You could sell it at a profit.'

'No,' said Harry. 'Now listen. Like I say, I've been thinking about what happened to Nick.'

'I wish I could help.'

'Then try and remember — was he ever in any bother? Anything at all?'

Derek shook his head. 'I have tried to remember. Believe me, I have.'

'You must have known straight away that the murder wasn't anything to do with the arcade. In fact, you were the only one that did know.'

Derek glanced to check the door was closed, then admitted, 'Course I was, yes. And I felt terrible about it, absolutely terrible.' But not terrible enough to tell the police, thought Harry. Save them wasting their time searching for the mysterious saboteur. 'But he always seemed as though he hadn't a care in the world, did Nick. A young man like that.' He winced and put a hand to his stomach. 'And he had his health.'

'Not for long,' said Harry.

'No, well . . . I don't think I'd notice a bullet in my guts, the pain I get.' The telephone began to ring. ''Scuse me,' he said to Harry, and answered it. 'Winter Gardens . . . ?'

Harry looked at the papers spread on the table. They were

covered in figures, the returns from each machine as far as he could judge. There were many crossings-out and alterations.

'For you,' said Derek, handing him the receiver.

'Thanks,' said Harry, then, into the phone, 'Hello?'

'Harry, it's me. Can you talk?'

It was Yvonne.

'Er, yes,' said Harry, moving as far from Derek as the telephone cord would allow. 'Just about, yes.'

'I'll leave you to it,' muttered Derek, taking the hint. And he left the office.

'OK,' said Harry, 'I can talk now. Did you find Salmon Gardens?'

'Yes. It's a big block of flats in South Kensington. Just off the Fulham Road. Quite nice ones too. Anyway I had a look round, then I went in and found number twenty-one.'

She paused, whether breathlessly or for effect Harry wasn't sure.

'Was anybody at home?'

'Yes, there was a woman inside. So I pretended to be looking for somebody else and to have got mixed up about the name.'

'Yes?'

'Well, that didn't get me very far. She couldn't wait to shut the door on me. In fact, she wasn't too keen on opening it in the first place. But I did notice one thing that was odd about her. She was wearing sun-glasses.'

At something of a loss, Harry said, 'Sun-glasses . . . ?'

'Well, don't you think that's strange? I mean it was quite dark. And there certainly wasn't any sun.'

He couldn't see that it mattered much, but didn't want to puncture Yvonne's enthusiasm with what she'd achieved.

'It does sound odd,' he said. 'But did you manage to get her name?'

'Well, not from her, no.' She was clearly intent on telling the full story.

'From somebody else then?' he asked patiently.

'Well, what I did — I went down to the main entrance and spoke to the porter. I pretended I'd been to the woman's flat to take an order for flowers. I thought flowers was a good idea.'

'Yes,' said Harry.

'And I pretended to have forgotten her name. Well, he was a bit reluctant to give it to me — it was against regulations and all that — but eventually he did.'

'And what was it?'

She told him.

'My God,' he said.

'Was it what you wanted?'

'It's, er . . . yes. Yes, thanks.'

'That's all right. I enjoyed it actually. Anyway, do you know yet when you're likely to be back?'

'Tomorrow,' he said, his mind elsewhere. 'I'll give you a ring.'

'All right,' she said. 'And let me know if there's anything else I can do, won't you?'

'Yes.'

'Well . . . bye then.'

'Bye.'

He realised she'd rung off and replaced his own receiver. Suddenly, after a morning of getting nowhere fast, had come a bolt from the blue. How big a bolt and quite what it signified he didn't yet know. But certainly Salmon Gardens SW7 was the address Nick had scribbled and Rose had seen.

As for the sun-glasses — they might have been no more than a silly affectation, but they, too, might yet turn out to be something more.

12

For a while after he'd finished talking to Yvonne, Harry remained in the office, needing to be alone and get one or two things clear. He had the tantalising feeling that the solution to Nick's murder was almost within his grasp and moving steadily nearer but that any false move on his part might lose it for ever.

He sat in Derek's chair, feet up on the table and hands clasped behind his head, and reconsidered all that he knew about the murder and about the history and character of the victim. To which could now be added what he knew about Salmon Gardens. And slowly, though still with questions unanswered and doubts unresolved, an idea began to emerge.

It wasn't an idea he particularly welcomed since it seemed wild and dangerous. Certainly not the sort he could hand over to the police without any evidence to support it.

In search of such evidence, he left the office and approached Reg.

'You remember the night Nick was killed?' he asked quietly.

'I do,' said Reg. 'Be a long time before I forget it.'

'What time did he go off-duty?'

'Oh, 'bout six. Perhaps a bit later.'

'Did he say anything about what he was going to do or where he was going?'

'Not a dicky-bird. I'd have told the cops if he had. They already asked me that.'

'Which way did he go when he left the arcade?'

Reg shook his head. 'No idea. I wasn't paying particular attention.' Then he added, 'Anyway, you were here, weren't you? What're you asking me for?'

It was a fair question. 'I was in the back,' admitted Harry. 'So I didn't see him go. I just thought you might have remembered something he said. . . ?'

'Well, I didn't, no. The only thing I remember was you saying you'd had a phone-call and so had to go down to the station to meet your young lady.'

Harry nodded. It was what he'd remembered, too: how he'd gone along the promenade, through the blanketing mist that had so suddenly descended, delaying Jill's train and making him sip coffee in the station buffet till she'd appeared.

Anyone superstitious might well be tempted to interpret such a weird phenomenon as an omen of the tragedy to come: the heavens themselves showing their distress. Someone less superstitious — such as Harry — might equally well be tempted to wonder whether there might not be a less fanciful, more prosaic connection.

He came to Derek, who was standing forlornly by the test-your-strength machine.

'Can I ask you something?'

'I'd have thought you already knew everything there was to know.'

'No, this is nothing to do with the arcade. Only, since I don't know the area like you do, I thought you could give me some advice.'

Derek looked at him curiously. 'What?'

'Suppose I wanted to take flying lessons?' Derek's eyebrows rose in surprise. 'Where would I go? Where's the nearest airport that might do something like that?'

'You want to learn how to fly?' asked Derek in disbelief.

'Not necessarily. But what if I did? Where would I go?'

'But I thought you were off back to London tomorrow? How're you going to learn to fly before then?'

Harry gave a patient smile and persisted: 'I'm just saying if. If I wanted to learn. Where would I go? Where's the nearest airport?'

Derek shrugged. Clearly he would never understand it so what was the point in trying?

'Lashingham,' he said simply. 'There's an airport at Lashingham. I dare say they do that sort of thing.'

'And how far's that?'

'Oh . . . be about fifteen miles. Can't be much further.'

'Thanks.'

'A pleasure,' said Derek, with a little laugh and a shake of the head. 'Let me know if there's anything else I can do. So long as you don't want me to come up with you as co-pilot.'

'I promise I won't ask you to do that,' smiled Harry. Then: 'Though there is just one other thing.'

'Oh yes, and what's that?' asked Derek, thrown back on the defensive.

'The car.'

'What car? My car?'

'Yes, the Rover. You said you were going to have to sell it and would I be interested.'

'I did, yes.'

'Well, now I've had time to think about it — it might not be such a bad idea after all.'

Derek looked at him, now clearly beginning to suspect his sanity.

'Are you serious?'

'Course I am. Are you serious about selling it?'

'Oh, I'm serious all right. Got no choice, have I?'

'Only I want another look at it first. And a test drive.'

'Any time,' said Derek, still bewildered.

'Well, I've only got today,' said Harry. 'Like you said, I'm not going to be here tomorrow, so . . .'

Happy to take the hint, Derek fished out a set of car-keys and handed them over. 'You know where it's parked. Be my guest.'

'Cheers.'

'Just what's got into you, though? Flying . . . ? New car . . . ? You come into a fortune all of a sudden?'

Harry smiled. He was wondering himself whether it was madness or inspiration that was behind his conduct. They said there wasn't much to choose between the two, and now he could believe it.

'Are you feeling all right?' persisted Derek.

'Quite all right, thank you,' said Harry, and left the arcade before he could be questioned further.

Lashingham airport struck Jill as quaint and old-fashioned, a place where people went to fly rather than to become inanimate bits of cargo, impersonal and in transit. More airfield than airport. The planes standing around were modest and sported propellers. The buildings were simple and few. An orange airsock indicated the direction of the breeze.

Not that arriving there brought her any nearer understanding why they'd come. The minute Harry had met her for lunch she could tell something had happened. There was an excitement and purposefulness about him that hadn't been there earlier and slightly frightened her.

'Where are we going?' she'd asked, as he'd packed her into Derek Underhill's Rover and driven out of St Stephen's Bay into the surrounding countryside.

'Oh, I just thought we'd find somewhere new to eat for a change.'

She'd let it go at that until they came to a junction and he'd pulled up and consulted a map before proceeding.

'I think there's something you're not telling me.'

'Why should you think that?'

'Well, why are we in this car for one thing?'

'I borrowed it.'

'And why're you looking at that map?'

'I borrowed that as well.'

Eventually they'd reached a pub that advertised food, though the abrupt way he braked and pulled off the road on to its carpark convinced her that this wasn't the object of their journey at all but simply somewhere he'd spotted in passing.

'What's going on, Harry?' she'd asked when they were settled with their ploughman's lunches.

'Who says there's anything going on?'

'I do.'

'I just thought you might enjoy a drive out.'

'I'd enjoy it more if I knew where we were going.'

'Derek Underhill wants to sell me his car.'

'And you're going to buy it?' she'd asked in surprise.

'No. But he was dead keen I should take it for a test drive so I thought well, why not? It can't do any harm, can it?'

She still didn't believe a word but had let it pass, knowing that sooner or later they'd reach their destination and she'd see it for herself. Harry ate quickly, eager to be off; she asked for a second drink, taking a small, perverse pleasure in delaying him.

Back on the road, her suspicions had been confirmed. With one eye on his map, Harry took them, not back towards St Stephen's Bay, but further in the opposite direction. Then had come a sign saying 'Airport', with a directing arrow. She said nothing till they reached a second arrow and the matter seemed beyond all reasonable doubt.

'We're going to an airport?'

'Yes. If you don't mind.'

'I mind not being told about it.'

'Sorry. It's just something I want to check on, that's all.'

And now here they were, strolling towards the small departure-lounge and halting together to watch the take-off of a single-seater aircraft that seemed to accelerate for no more than a few yards before climbing into the skies. She gazed after it till it was the size of a toy, then saw that Harry was looking around as though in search of something.

'What are you looking for?'

'Oh, nothing in particular. Let's go in here, shall we?'

They found a door that admitted them to what was more of a waiting-room than departure-lounge. There were doors off marked 'Customs', 'Enquiries' and 'Lashingham Flying Club'. In one corner a woman sat beside a small mobile canteen. Also present were two men, oily and overalled, who were drinking tea and discussing something technical.

'Sit down,' said Harry.

'I'd rather find a loo.'

'Shall I get you a cup of tea for when you come back?'

'If you like,' she said, becoming exasperated by his mysterious manner. All right, she'd gone along this far, playing the obedient companion, asking no questions — well, hardly any — and being told a load of half-lies, but now they'd arrived and wasn't it time she was allowed to know a little more about . . . well, about whatever there was to know about? But first she needed a loo, and so went to find one while he approached the woman with the tea-urn.

When she returned, he wasn't there.

'I think this is for you, dear,' called the woman, holding out a cup of tea.

'Oh, is it? Thank you.'

'The gentleman said he'd be back in a minute.'

'Did he pay for this?' asked Jill, taking the cup.

'Oh yes.'

Gracious of him, she thought, flopping down on to one of the black, vinyl-covered seats. He pays for a cup of tea, then buggers off, leaving her to drink it. What was she doing here anyway? What was she doing with him at all? As if on cue, the old doubts began to resurface.

As a couple they were as different as chalk and cheese. She couldn't remember why she'd ever gone out with him in the first place. Or how those first meetings — mostly fiascos of one sort or another — had paved the way for them to become joint lease-holders of a new flat. She didn't know which she disliked the most: the times when he kowtowed to her every opinion, never arguing with her, accepting her every utterance as better informed and therefore superior to his; or the times like this, when he told her nothing but dragged her along as though she were some dumb blonde of a side-kick, decorative but untrustworthy.

She got to her feet. 'Which way did he go?' she asked the woman.

'Oh, along there,' she said, indicating a corridor. 'But he said he'd be back in a minute.'

'Thanks,' said Jill shortly, and went down the corridor in pursuit.

There were a couple of doors, one locked, the other admitting her to a broom-cupboard, and then she was at the end, with a glass door between herself and the outside world. It was unlocked. She pushed it open and went through, finding herself facing a semi-circle of hangars with planes parked here and there before them. Away to her right a small group of men in suits and carrying briefcases was filing on to one of the larger aircraft, otherwise there was little sign of life. And no sign of Harry.

'Oh, for God's sake . . . !' she said aloud.

It occurred to her to repay him in kind and walk off as he'd done. More dramatically, to catch a plane back to London and leave him to work that one out. Though really, of course, she had to wait, standing around and feeling slightly foolish, till he should choose to show up.

The thought of London made her wonder what they'd find there on their return. She'd come to St Stephen's Bay to escape the attentions of Greg and to carry news of his threat to Harry. Presumably they'd return to find that threat being put into effect and would one day soon be reading about the hapless private eye and his criminal past. And then what? Would the bad publicity force the agency to close, leaving Harry without a job, unemployable save by the gangsters he'd known before? And leaving her . . . where? Impossible to answer.

And then she saw him, coming from a small, prefabricated building that stood beside one of the hangars. It had a sign on the front — 'Mercury Airways' — with other announcements and what might have been time-tables below it, though these she was too far away to see.

He spotted her, gave a wave and headed towards her. She didn't respond, letting him see her displeasure. The big oaf, she thought, watching him duck under the wing of an aircraft. Doing his best to solve other people's problems and probably, in his own haphazard way, doing his best to keep her happy too. You couldn't help but love him even if you kicked yourself for doing so.

'Sorry about that,' he called as he approached.

'So you should be.'

'I just had to check on something. Did you get your cup of tea?'

'Yes.'

'Great. Well, we'll get back now, shall we?'

But she didn't move. Even dumb blondes have to make a stand occasionally.

'Harry, what is going on?'

He stepped close to her and took her face in his hands.

'I'll tell you tomorrow.'

'Tell me now,' she insisted.

'No.'

'Why not?'

He sighed, then, seeing she wasn't going to be put off so easily, dropped his hands and said in a more serious tone, 'I can't tell you what's going on because I don't know myself yet.'

'Then what are we doing here? What have you been doing just now?'

'I've been making some enquiries.' She gave a tut of annoyance at the familiar, meaningless jargon. 'Well, I have. I'm still working for Derek Underhill, remember. I finish tomorrow. And then I'll tell you all about it.'

'Oh, all right,' she said, giving up. 'We might as well get back then.' And she marched away across the tarmac before him. Let him follow in her footsteps; she wasn't going to give him the satisfaction of following meekly in his.

They continued that way for another fifty yards till she could no longer hear his footsteps behind her and glanced round to see what had happened. He'd disappeared. Once again he'd disappeared.

'Over here.'

His voice brought her head round, even as her fury was growing. There he was, away to her left, and grinning broadly. Behind him a sign said 'Car-Park'. She'd been going in the wrong direction.

He now knew who'd killed Nick Wyatt. And he knew why. What he didn't know was how to prove it. He still had neither witnesses nor evidence and little prospect of coming across either.

He could, of course, go and talk to Superintendent Charlton and hope to convince him that here was the truth and not just the desperate imaginings of a weary private eye. Tell him about Salmon Gardens. And about the airport. And then leave it to him to trawl those murky waters in search of witnesses and evidence.

It was an option he decided to hold in reserve, a last resort for tomorrow morning before they left. In the meantime there was still tonight.

He returned the car to Derek and said he'd had second thoughts about buying it. 'It's a bit heavy on the old petrol.'

'Only if you drive it,' said Derek. 'You leave it stood outside and it'll cost you nothing.'

But he didn't seem resentful. Perhaps he was past being resentful at anything much.

'I won't be in the arcade tonight. I've got some business,' said Harry. 'But I'll be in to see you tomorrow, OK?'

'Suit yourself.'

Jill, the other person he had to take into his plans, seemed to have forgiven him the liberties of the afternoon. He knew he'd been skating on thin ice, taking her all the way to the airport and then leaving her alone there with never more than the minimum of explanation. There hadn't, though, been any alternative. Now all he asked was that she should put up with one last night of his mysterious ways.

'I thought we'd celebrate,' he said.

'Oh yes, and what's that supposed to mean?'

'Dinner at the Imperial.'

'Is that the grotty hotel along the promenade?'

'It's not all that grotty,' he protested. 'At least it's the best of a bad lot.'

'Exactly.'

He knew it wouldn't be to her liking. Her preference was for the discreet and the small-scale while the Imperial, like the Winter Gardens, was another relic of the town's grandiose past, though one better preserved and still functioning. It stood on the seaward side of the promenade, in need of repainting and in uncomfortable proximity to the fairground across the road.

'Just for one last night,' he persisted. 'I'd like to go there. I like the look of the place.'

She regarded him and shook her head sadly. 'All right,' she said, humouring him. 'If it's as important as all that. Let's go and get it over with.'

They came down the thirty-nine steps, past the brass gong, and out into a night that was threatening more rain.

'I'll get us a taxi,' he said, since neither of them had a coat.

'There's no need.'

'There might be in a minute.'

She continued to insist it wasn't necessary as he continued to peer in vain up and down the promenade in search of a cruising taxi, until they'd arrived at the Imperial without either finding one or getting wet. Laughing about it, they went up the wide steps and through the swing doors.

The hotel surprised Harry — and Jill too, though she wouldn't admit it — by being busier and better run than its neglected façade had given them the right to expect. They were shown into a large dining-room, full of hunting pictures in gilt frames, its tables laid with heavy silver cutlery and cut glass.

'I bet we're the only ones here not on a dirty weekend,' said Jill, looking around them.

'I thought we were on one. Well, sort of, anyway.'

She eyed him. 'Are you trying to get at me?'

'No.'

'Oh.' And she gave an apologetic smile. 'Only I know you wanted this to be a holiday for us and, well, what with one thing and another . . . it hasn't been much of one, has it?'

'There's time yet,' he promised her solemnly.

The waiter arrived and they fell to studying a menu that was conservatively English and a disappointment after the cutlery.

They were both hungry, though, and ate well. It was only while waiting for dessert that she noticed him taking a surreptitious glance at his watch.

'If I didn't know you better,' she said slowly, 'I'd say you had an ulterior motive for bringing me here.'

'And what on earth would that be?'

'I don't know. Just that you seem very concerned with keeping track of the time.'

'Sorry,' he said lightly. 'I just wasn't sure whether my watch was working. It's been doing some funny things this week.'

'You're a liar,' she said, smiling. 'There's nothing wrong with your bloody watch. And the only funny thing about this week has been the way you've been behaving.'

Stuck for words, he gave a small laugh, then busied himself with the dessert that, mercifully, had arrived at last. Coffee, they were informed, was served in the lounge, and it was to there they retired when the meal was over.

At least the lounge boasted a clock: he needn't risk drawing more scornful comment by checking his watch. It showed nine-thirty — time he made a move. Before which he must run the greater risk of making a confession.

'You were right,' he said.

'About what?'

'I did have, you know . . . whatever-you-called-it . . . '

'An ulterior motive.'

'Yes. For bringing you here. I did have one, yes.'

'What?'

'I've got some business to attend to. Near here.'

'What sort of business?'

'Confidential.' She gave a groan of dismay. He hurried on. 'It shouldn't take long, but I'll have to leave you for a while. And I thought here was somewhere I could leave you and you'd be all right on your own.'

'That was nice of you,' she said coolly.

'What I'll do, I'll pay for the meal now. Then you can stay here, order drinks, whatever you like . . . and I'll be back before you know it.'

She made him wait for her response so that for a moment he feared a scene. Perhaps this time he really had pushed her too far.

'Sorry,' he said. 'I'll tell you all about it afterwards.'

She gave a sigh of resignation and said mockingly, 'You know, you're so predictable.' Then opened her handbag and produced a paperback copy of *Far From the Madding Crowd*, that he recognised as the one she was currently in the middle of reading.

'Oh,' he said in surprise. 'You expected it?'

'I didn't know what to expect. It's a case of being prepared.'

He gave her a smile of gratitude, kissed her swiftly and said, 'I'll see you soon.'

'Be careful.'

'I will.'

And he was at last able to leave her and embark on the real business of the evening.

It meant leaving, too, the faded gentility of the Imperial, waiting for a gap in the traffic, crossing the promenade and entering into the raucous din of the fairground where the lights were blazing and everything was still in full swing. At first he simply wandered between the stalls and the rides, losing himself in the crowd. Then, as if by accident, found himself arriving at the fairground office from where Charlie Monroe ruled over his seaside empire.

There was a light on upstairs, but that mattered little since it was too soon yet to consider entering. What he wanted to know was how such an entry might later be managed. He scouted round the two-storey, red-bricked building. There were bars over the windows at the back and the silver strips of a burglar alarm over those at the front. The door had at least one deadlock besides the Yale.

He drew back from the building, still trying to look as though he were sauntering aimlessly instead of casing it. He hadn't expected it to be easy but had hoped that a way in would somehow present itself. His options were either to try and con his way inside − helped by the selection of cards he carried in his inside pocket, identifying him as everything from security consultant to magazine salesman, that he'd one day discovered in Clifford Humphries' old desk − which might work if the person currently inside the office were anyone other than Charlie Monroe but certainly wouldn't work if it turned out to be Charlie himself, or he could wait until the fairground had emptied and attempt burglary, which wasn't one of his particular skills despite a long acquaintance with many masters in the art.

Or he could walk away and do nothing.

To give himself time to decide, and the fairground time to clear, he wandered to a nearby shooting-gallery and had eight shots for fifty pence. The result wasn't exactly disgraceful, a close grouping around the inner target, but wasn't enough to win him one of the outsized, fluffy teddy-bears offered as prizes. Probably a good thing, too. The burglary option, were he to go for it, wouldn't be helped by his having to take a large, furry friend along with him.

The stalls were now beginning to put up their shutters and the crowds to drift towards the exits. The lights along the track of the Big Dipper went out and its amplified music fell silent. It was as though night were suddenly falling, not gracefully with a spreading sunset but at the abrupt decision of the management.

Harry studied the outside of the office block, feeling himself under pressure of time and needing to come to a decision. Suppose he went straight in through one of the front windows, counting on being able to cut off the alarm once he was inside. The gamble would be whether anyone would react to the alarm before he could silence it. And whether he could find what he was after before they did.

It was a gamble he never had to take. The issue was simply and heart-stoppingly resolved for him as he stood contemplating the building and trying to make up his mind.

'Well, well, well,' said a voice behind him. 'If it isn't my old friend, Harry Sommers.'

He didn't have to turn to know it was Charlie Monroe and that all his plans were suddenly beside the point.

'Evening, Charlie,' he said evenly.

'I thought I might find you here.'

Why, thought Harry. Then was told.

'There I was, having a quiet drink in the Imperial Hotel. And lo and behold, who should I see but that lady-friend of yours, all alone and reading a book. So naturally my first thought was — where the hell has Harry got to?'

Harry silently cursed his carelessness. He'd been too concerned with finding a comfortable spot where Jill might be left to guess that her presence in the Imperial might betray him.

'So now you've found me,' he said lightly.

'Now I've found you. Taking more than a passing interest in my office by the looks of things.'

'Not particularly.'

'Well, it seems so to me. Would you like to look inside? Might as well since you've come this far, eh?'

Harry hesitated. There were dangers in this invitation he couldn't foresee. Still, as Charlie said, he'd come this far and so might as well.

'All right. Why not.'

'Why not indeed,' said Charlie, and laid a hand on his shoulder. It stayed there as they walked together to the building and went in through the front door.

'Up there,' said Charlie, indicating a flight of stairs. Harry went first and found himself in a neon-lit office. Behind a desk at its centre, a small man in a donkey-jacket looked up at him in surprise and tried to hide a pornographic magazine.

'All right, Phil?' said Charlie, following Harry in.

'Mr Monroe,' said Phil, getting hastily to his feet. 'I wasn't expecting you.'

'Course you weren't. Now piss off, will you.'

'Right, yes. Thanks, Mr Monroe.'

And he scuttled out of the office.

Charlie closed the door.

'Sit down,' he said to Harry. 'Make yourself at home.'

Harry perched cautiously on the edge of a chair. Charlie went to the other side of the desk and lowered himself into the leather armchair recently vacated by Phil, observing Harry but saying nothing. Harry gazed around the walls, which were adorned by framed photographs of Charlie in the company of smiling celebrities — and of a more recent vintage than those displayed by Gypsy Rose — a couple of certificates testifying to his membership of something-or-other and a dart-board with three darts stuck in the bull's-eye.

Charlie spoke at last. 'You like fun-fairs, do you, Harry?'

Harry shrugged. 'I can take 'em or leave 'em.'

'Well, it strikes me you must be very keen. Abandoning your lady-friend like that.'

'She prefers reading.'

'Lucky you. My wife — she prefers spending.'

Another pause. Let him make the running, Harry told himself. He can't be sure how much I know or if I really know anything. That's why he wants to talk.

'Why're you so interested in my office all of a sudden, Harry?'
'Who says I am?'
'I say you are. I watched you sniffing around. What are you looking for, Harry? What are you after?'
'Nothing,' said Harry stubbornly.
'I said I wanted you out of this town.'
'So you did.'
'But you haven't gone, have you? That's always been your trouble, Harry. Pig-headed. Can't take advice.'
'You might be right.'
'I know I'm right. And I'll tell you something else I know as well, shall I? I know where you were this afternoon.'
'Oh yes?' said Harry, trying to sound casual, though in truth shaken and knowing suddenly that the trouble he'd sought to avoid was coming at him hard and fast.
'Lashington airport,' said Charlie.
'I had a drive round there, yes.'
'And why was that?'
'No particular reason. Watch the aeroplanes.'
Charlie shook his head and gave a grim smile. 'I don't think you're being altogether honest, are you, Harry boy? See, I have friends there. And they've been telling me that you were making some rather pointed enquiries.'
Harry sat silent. What friends, he wondered. Presumably the man he'd spoken to in the Mercury Airways office. Who'd seen fit to get on the phone and tell Charlie there'd been a strange character asking even stranger questions about him.
So Charlie did know how much he knew. Knew that it was everything.
'I didn't know you was interested in planes, Harry?'
'You'd be surprised what I'm interested in.'
'Oh, I would, would I?'
Slowly and with an exaggerated care, he took a bunch of keys from his pockets, selected one, and used it to unlock the top

drawer of his desk. He opened the drawer, reached in and, to Harry's surprise and alarm, produced a gun. A small, modern-looking pistol which he held so that it was pointing across the desk and at Harry's chest.

'What about this, Harry? Would you be interested in this?'

13

Of the many things that crossed Harry's mind at the sight of the gun, the first was an image of the severed head of a donkey lying in a bath.

It was Nick, of course, who'd told him the tale. Proof, if proof were ever needed, of how Charlie Monroe could switch from golf club bon viveur to violent lunatic at the drop of a hat. He'd been a madman five years earlier when he'd employed Harry in his London club, flying off the handle at every imagined slight and scoffing at the caution and conservatism of the underworld figures he met. Till he'd lost a lot of money and gone home, relieving his frustrations by hacking the heads off donkeys.

From which he'd progressed to the killing of Nick Wyatt.

'This is what you were looking for, is it?' he said, waggling the gun.

'Yes,' said Harry, throwing caution to the winds. His only chance now was to stop pussyfooting about. Try and convince Charlie that too much was already known about Nick's murder for shooting him to make a ha'p'orth of difference.

Charlie nodded. 'I thought as much. I thought it when I saw you hanging about outside there. I even thought it when I saw your tart parked on her tod over the road.'

Harry shifted on his chair, trying to relax. Stay calm, he told himself. Stay calm and clear-headed. He even managed a smile.

'Don't try anything,' said Charlie, suddenly alarmed. 'Don't get any clever ideas or I'll blow your bleeding brains out.'

He pulled his tie loose and opened the collar of his shirt. There were beads of sweat on his forehead and the hand holding the gun trembled when he lifted it from the desk. Charlie wasn't calm, Harry decided. Charlie wasn't a bit calm.

'Just think a minute,' said Harry quietly. 'Just think what you're doing.'

'I know what I'm doing all right.'

'What?'

'I'm going to stop you once and for all, that's what.'

'You're going to shoot me?'

'Probably, yes. Why? That doesn't worry you, does it?'

Harry felt the sweat running from his own brow. This staying calm routine wasn't easy, not when your adversary announced he was going to shoot you and you knew he meant it.

'That would be stupid,' said Harry. 'That'd be about the stupidest thing you could do.'

'Well, you would think that. But then you've got rather a biased point of view, wouldn't you say?'

'People know I'm here.'

'Oh yes? Like who for example?'

'Like Jill. The woman in the hotel. She knows I'm here.'

Charlie took a moment to consider then, with the shrewdness of the half-crazed, delivered his opinion: 'Well no, see, I don't believe she does. 'Cause I don't believe you would have told her. Tarts like her don't want to know about the nasty bits. They want to be left alone with their books while you're out getting your hands dirty.'

It wasn't a bad analysis.

Rather than contest it, Harry played another card from his rather thin hand. 'The police are interested in you, Charlie. You know they are. Wasn't that what you got all steamed up at me about?'

'The police *was* interested, yes. But not any more they're not.'

'They would be if I got shot.'

'Well, that would depend. For one thing, it'd depend on where you were at the time. And where the gun happened to get itself found.'

'Come on, Charlie,' said Harry as steadily as he could, 'you're not going to get away with it. Why not cut your losses? Put the gun away, let's talk it over and see what we can do for the best.'

But Charlie's imagination had been fired. 'I might always say it was your gun. And that I went to grab it off you and there was this terrible accident where you ended up shooting yourself.'

'You'd be wasting your breath. Nobody's going to believe that.'

'Oh, they might. 'Specially if I had witnesses. Like Phil for instance. You saw little Phil that was in here when we came in? Now I bet he could remember seeing you with a gun in your hand if he tried hard enough.'

He probably could, thought Harry. He'd known enough such cases where a combination of money and fear had played strange tricks with the memories of witnesses.

'But why would I do that?' he countered. 'Why would I be coming after you with a gun?'

Charlie shrugged. 'Thousand and one reasons. I mean we aren't exactly the best of mates, are we? And there's one or two people might remember that little barney we had outside that crematorium place.'

True.

'And where am I supposed to have got the gun from?' persisted Harry, without much hope.

'Anywhere. I mean a private eye down from the big city where it's all vice and corruption. Bound to have a gun, aren't you?'

'The same gun that was used to shoot Nick . . . ?'

Charlie hesitated, then nodded. 'It might turn out that way, yes. But then that's not going to do your reputation much good, is it?'

Harry shrugged. The conversation felt futile. Charlie was toying with him, killing time.

He doesn't want to shoot me here, he realised. Despite his bluster about being able to provide witnesses to order, he doesn't want a body on the premises if it can be avoided. Was it then to be the tried-and-tested formula by which he'd disposed of Nick? Take his victim for a walk on the promenade and rely on the tide to clear up after him?

'See, you're too clever for your own good, Harry boy. Always have been.'

'So you said.'

'It wasn't only me. There's others have said it as well. You think you're smarter than the people who employ you, and you're not, 'cause if you were you'd be making the money they are and it'd be you that'd be employing them.'

He was rabbiting on, reasoned Harry, till he could be sure the fairground would be deserted, with neither punters nor employees on hand to see them walk to the car.

'I mean look at the money I make and then look at what you do. And then ask yourself who's the smart one, eh? Is it you? Are you really all that bleeding smart?'

'No,' said Harry.

'Too right you're not. Hey . . .'

The cry was one of alarm as he slid from his leather armchair and landed heavily on the floor, halfway under his desk and with Harry still hanging on to his feet. It was the kind of desk with an opening at the front through which you could stretch your legs, as Charlie had been doing before Harry had ducked down, grabbed both ankles and up-ended him.

It didn't, though, release his hold on the gun which was somewhere down there with him. Deciding not to stand on ceremony, Harry was out through the door before Charlie could resurface. He went down the stairs three at a time and came to the door at the bottom which — thank God — was held only by its Yale lock. He released the latch and then was outside and running.

The looming structures that were the closed-up stalls and rides provided cover and gave him time to think. His first reaction was to keep going, collect Jill, and then keep going still further. It was an almost overwhelming temptation, and yet . . . He'd achieved nothing of what he'd come for. The gun for which he'd been searching was there all right but he'd failed to bring it out with him. All he'd done, in fact, was to alert Charlie to the dangers of hanging on to it. By tomorrow morning it'd be safely buried in the silt of the English Channel.

A shot rang out and he flattened himself against the nearest wall. Peering round it, he saw a figure silhouetted against the open door through which he'd made his escape. Whether he'd been seen by Charlie he couldn't tell. The shot might have been a wild one, a warning.

It meant, though, that the quick getaway was no longer on the cards. He'd paused too long for that and now had to retreat as the figure of Charlie left the office doorway and came towards him. He edged his way around the rough-hewn building, recognising it now as the shooting-gallery he'd patronised earlier. Amazing how quickly shooting lost its appeal once you became the target.

A can went clattering away from beneath his foot. Sod it, he thought. Seen or not, he must now have been heard. As if in confirmation, there was another shot, then the sound of footsteps quickly approaching. Harry turned, trying to duck and run at the same time. Dark and deserted, the fairground had suddenly become a maze, offering cover of all shapes and sizes but where Charlie held the invaluable advantage of being on familiar territory.

Scurrying away from his pursuer and without time to consider where he was heading, Harry found a low wall across his path. He took a quick glance at what seemed to be a smooth, even surface on the other side of it, and vaulted over. He landed with a splash and found himself up to his knees in water. It was such a shock he stood stock-still for a moment, bewildered. Water . . . ? Where was he for Christ's sake? And all the time, behind him, Charlie was approaching. He must have heard the splash and so would know more about where Harry was than Harry knew himself.

Unable to go back, he waded forward. Before him rose a wall of rock that, as he got nearer, revealed itself to be the entrance to a cave. The pitch darkness inside gave no clue to its depth though the receding echoes of Harry's splashing about suggested it might be considerable. Impossible, though, to assess whether what he was being offered here was safe hiding-place or deadly cul-de-sac.

Then he saw that Charlie had arrived. No more than thirty yards away and looking, it seemed, straight at him. He can't see me, thought Harry. I'm in darkness and he can't see me. Then his arm came up as though to aim and Harry thought oh shit, yes he can, and waded quickly forward into the darkness. A shot splashed into the water behind him.

It was like a bad dream, running through water, using all his energies yet managing little more than a slow-motion stagger. And still with the fear that he'd come eventually to a dead-end.

Then, even as the darkness was beginning to seem welcoming and protective, it had gone. Lights came on around him, not powerful but subdued and hidden, showing him a stretch of water reaching ahead and strange grottos all around. He knew at last where he was. He was in the Tunnel of Love.

Beside him, a group of plastic rabbits gambolled on plastic grass. Ten yards ahead, on the other side, a small palm-tree supported coconuts and a grinning monkey.

From behind came a new sound he couldn't at first identify. Though, whatever it was, it was gaining fast and he began again his desperate, clumsy rush forward. Oars, he realised. That had been the new sound of pursuit. Charlie Monroe was coming after him by boat.

He scanned each grotto as he waded past it — the palm-tree, then a miniature Eros on a miniature fountain — but none offered any real chance of concealment. On impulse he grabbed at the figure of Eros and wrenched it from its base. He turned and hurled it back down the tunnel, then hurried on with no time to stay and observe. Though it was gratifying a moment later to hear a shot ring out. Charlie had plugged the floating Eros and Harry had gained a few seconds' respite.

He saw the end of the tunnel and splashed towards it. The

sound of the oars resumed behind him. Finally he was out and in the open. Another low wall marked the water's edge. He pulled himself over it and was back on dry land. Wet, weary and desperate.

He still didn't know where he was or in which direction to run. Ahead of him he could make out the massive skeleton of the Big Dipper. Wasn't that somewhere near the fairground's entrance? He hurried towards it. Behind him, Charlie's boat emerged from the tunnel, then came the sound of splashing and bumping as Charlie abandoned it and followed Harry on to terra firma.

Harry moved further in among the girders that supported the Big Dipper, its track a giant knot of curves and bends above him. He now saw he'd been right in thinking it near the entrance. The trouble was he'd gone and boxed himself in, coming up against the tall fence topped with barbed-wire that marked the fairground's perimeter. The entrance might as well have been on the far side of the moon, for Charlie Monroe, gun in hand and advancing slowly, was blocking all possible escape in that direction.

Decision time again. He couldn't remain forever hidden beneath the Big Dipper. Its ironwork cast confusing shadows but wouldn't give much cover once Charlie spotted him. Harry dodged backwards between the metal stanchions. Charlie had stopped and was staring hard — with that unfocused stare that said he couldn't yet see what he was looking for. Harry continued to edge slowly away from him — though there wasn't much further he could go — and tried to control his breathing, which was so loud in his own ears it was incredible Charlie couldn't hear it too.

Close to him, the track dipped to no more than head height and brought with it an idea. If only he could hoist himself up on to it, he'd not only be a more difficult target, becoming more so the higher he went, but he could then follow the track round to where it swung out over the perimeter fence and there drop from it to safety.

He grasped the edge of the track above him, then pulled

himself up till he could swing first one foot up and then his whole body so that he was finally on the track, lying flat, six feet up, and waiting with bated breath to see whether his exertions had alerted Charlie.

Apparently not. He was still peering in, among the supports, reluctant to come forward without first catching sight of his prey. Which he was bound to do once Harry started to climb. His only protection then would be the boarding that supported the metal track. Crawling would be slow and, anyway, noisy. He had to risk getting to his feet and taking the first incline at a run, hoping to get far enough up before Charlie could line up a clear shot.

He counted to three, told himself to go, hesitated, and then finally did go. His every step clattered on the boards but there was no avoiding that. He made ten, then twenty yards, came to the first incline where he had to grasp the rail with his hands, hauling himself up while being careful to keep his feet clear of the chain with its protruding teeth that ran between the tracks and hoisted the cars to the top.

Thirty-five feet above ground, he was now reaching the summit. The track flattened ahead of him before beginning its fall. Don't look down, Harry told himself. Suddenly a shot rang out and ricocheted somewhere beneath him. Now at the top, he lay still, feeling safe from Charlie though not from the drop ahead of him. Was it better to go down backwards, as down a ladder, or to slide down forwards? Once down, he then had another, smaller hill to climb before the track swung out over the wire and he'd be able to make his escape.

Faint footsteps reached him from below. By the sound of them they were going away, though he didn't yet dare hope that Charlie was giving up. He waited but heard nothing more. Peering down, he could see no sign of his enemy.

Suddenly the whole structure shuddered. Harry grabbed at the rails in alarm. Then came the rumble of machinery from below. Oh no, pleaded Harry, knowing instantly what it meant: Charlie had switched on the power that fed the track and any moment now would be climbing up towards him in one of the cars.

The noise changed to a harsher whine and he knew without having to look that the metal teeth had been engaged and were dragging Charlie up. Or anyway were dragging a car up. Whether Charlie was in it remained to be seen. Might he not be content to wait below till Harry was dislodged from his perch?

No. One glance told Harry otherwise. A single, squat figure occupied the front seat of the car as it rose through the gloom towards him.

Harry scrambled to his feet and threw himself recklessly forward, half-sliding, half-falling down the track, grabbing at the rail to slow his descent. He lost his footing, regained it, lost it again, then, as the track began to level, he was upright and running. Behind him, the bulk of the car attained the summit, stood poised for a moment on the brink, then came charging after him down the slope.

It would hit him long before he could get up the next incline. He caught a glimpse of Charlie leaning forward with his gun, and jumped.

His sense of relief that the car had missed him was swallowed by fear as the ground failed to arrive. Just how far up had be been for God's sake? Then, with a sickening jolt, he'd landed, his legs gave way and he sprawled full-length on the ground.

He lay for a moment, giving thanks, then tried to stand, an action that provoked an agonising pain in his left ankle and a not quite so agonising one in his right. Was either broken? Anyway, he had to move. He couldn't remain where he was with Charlie still swooping around the track and due to arrive back not twenty yards from where Harry now lay.

He managed to get to his feet, though the pain of doing so made him moan aloud. He limped forward, wondering whether he could make it out and to the promenade, then saw the control booth from where Charlie must have switched on the Big Dipper. Its door was standing open. Harry stopped, struck by a new set of possibilities. With Charlie's car still careering around the far reaches of the track, he had time to plan and, more importantly, the sure knowledge of where Charlie was and the point to which he'd be returning.

He went to the booth, forgetting the pain as he studied the controls, which covered several of the surrounding rides and attractions. Inside, too, were some tools, a couple of buckets, brooms and a spade.

His first idea was simply to switch the power off and leave his adversary stuck out on the track of the Big Dipper. That way he'd at least give himself time to hobble to safety. He raised his hands to the button then stopped. There was an alternative.

One-and-a-half minutes later Charlie's car came screaming down the final incline, slowed and came to a halt. There was no sign of Harry. Charlie remained where he was for a few moments, crouched in the front seat, gun at the ready. When nothing happened, he stepped cautiously from the car, taking a deep breath to calm the slight giddiness the ride had induced. He looked around, then began to move back towards the spot where Harry had jumped. Perhaps he'd still be there, unconscious or disabled — you never knew when you might get lucky.

Suddenly there was an explosion of light and a guffawing of laughter. He looked round frantically, bringing the gun to bear on the blue of a police uniform.

In the time it took for Charlie to register that someone had switched on the Laughing Policeman, Harry had covered the ground from behind the control booth and was swinging the spade he'd borrowed from inside it. His aim was spot on. The blade of the spade made satisfying, bone-crunching contact with the crown of Charlie Monroe's head. He gave a single grunt, his knees folded and he collapsed forward on to the ground.

Thrown off balance by the effort of the blow, Harry went down too. This time his ankle wouldn't support him so that he could do no more than raise himself to a sitting position.

Which was a good deal more than Charlie Monroe would be managing for some time. He was out cold. Blood was beginning to trickle from the wound in his scalp.

Then, through the continued guffawing of the Laughing Policeman, Harry became aware of approaching sirens. He waited. There were distant shouts and running feet, then figures materialised into the light. They were policemen, not laughing but wide-eyed at the strange scene. Two of them he recognised.

'My God,' exclaimed Sergeant Greer.

'Evening,' said Harry.

'What the hell's going on?' said Superintendent Charlton, eyeing the Laughing Policeman without a shadow of a smile.

'There's your murderer,' said Harry, indicating the still figure beside him. 'Check his gun. You'll find it's the one that did for Nick Wyatt.'

14

An hour later Harry was in the Casualty Department of St Stephen's Bay Memorial Hospital, awaiting the results of X-rays on both his ankles and escorted by Jill and two policemen.

Charlie Monroe, escorted by a considerably larger posse of policemen, had already been whisked through ahead of Harry. He'd had stitches inserted where the spade had split his scalp but not, as it turned out, his skull, and had then been removed at high speed to the local nick. In the meantime Superintendent Charlton had had a quick word with Harry and heard about why he'd ever begun to suspect Charlie Monroe and why, in particular, he'd gone to his office that evening. Now Jill, too, wanted to know.

'Well, the first thing,' said Harry, 'was when I realised that, whoever had shot Nick, it wasn't anything to do with the arcade.'

'And what made you realise that?'

He looked round to check that the waiting policemen couldn't overhear their conversation; nor, for that matter, that anyone else could. But no-one seemed to be paying much attention: the policemen were chatting up a nurse, while the night's other casualties, scattered amid the rows of stacking-chairs, all seemed preoccupied with their own sufferings.

Even so, he kept his voice down.

'It was Derek Underhill who was behind it all.'

'Behind all the . . . ?'

'Behind all the aggro, yes. He wanted to create the impression there was somebody out to cause bother for him. But there wasn't. Just him setting it up to look that way.'

'But then why did he call you in?'

'Because I was his ultimate alibi. He must have been innocent if he was going to the lengths of employing me to sort it all out.'

'Well, yes,' she conceded, 'I can see that. But why was he doing it in the first place?'

That was trickier, calling for the exercise of discretion. It wasn't a matter of protecting Derek's reputation so much as his own. Jill wouldn't be at all amused to learn how he'd connived at covering up attempted arson.

'Well, I'm not really sure. I think it's something to do with local rivalries.'

'And I think you're lying again,' she said, seeing through his evasion.

'No, really. I'm not sure just what he was up to, but it doesn't matter now. He knows he's been found out and won't try it on again.'

'And I still think you're lying,' she said. 'But I'll let you off seeing as you've got two wonky ankles and have made such a mess of your best suit.'

'Thanks.'

'But I still want to know how all that helped you solve the murder.'

'Well, it meant I had to start again from scratch,' explained Harry. 'Start thinking about Nick and the kind of person he was and what he might have been involved in.'

'So?'

'So I decided here was a young man, on his own, out to have a good time.'

'Brilliant,' she said, softening the sarcasm with a smile.

'Well, I'm not sure about that. But what I mean is — he was a chancer. He came down from Norwich with no job. Just hung around till he found one. And he was a great one for pulling the birds.'

She frowned at the phrase. 'You mean girls found him attractive.'

'Exactly. And he found them attractive as well I daresay.'

'And so what did you deduce from all that?'

'Well, not a lot,' he admitted. 'Not till later. It was Rose who gave me the real break.'

'Rose . . . ?'

'Gypsy Rose. The fortune-teller. She gave me an address —

twenty-one Salmon Gardens — that she'd seen Nick writing down.'

'Salmon Gardens where, though?'

'Ah well yes, that's the point. I started off thinking it must be local, somewhere round here. It was only when I realised that perhaps the murder wasn't anything to do with the arcade that it occurred to me it sounded more like a London address.'

'And was it?'

'Yes. Near South Ken. And guess who owned it.'

'No idea.'

'Yes, you have.'

She looked at him, thought a moment, then said, 'Ah.'

'You've guessed,' he said, smiling.

'Charlie Monroe . . . ?'

'Dead right. Mr and Mrs C. Monroe were listed as tenants. I got Yvonne to go round and check.'

'It must be wonderful to have women awaiting your every beck and call.'

'It must. Anyway, do you want to know the rest?'

'Yes.'

'Well, Yvonne went to the flat and actually talked to Mrs Monroe. Or at least tried to talk to her. She apparently wasn't very keen. And one thing she noticed was that Mrs Monroe was wearing sun-glasses.' Jill looked at him blankly. 'Well yes, I know. Lots of people do.'

'They do,' she agreed.

'But Yvonne thought it was odd when there wasn't too much light around this place. Which made me wonder — could she have been wearing them to hide a black eye?'

Jill nodded slowly. 'Good thinking, Watson.'

'Or even two black eyes?'

'Even better.'

'Which would have been another reason why Charlie would have wanted her up in London, out of the way. He wouldn't want her walking around St Stephen's Bay showing everybody what he'd done to her. And then I thought about the night that poor old Nick was shot.'

'The night I arrived on the train . . . ?'

'That's the one. When there was all the fog everywhere. I'd already been told that Charlie Monroe was in the habit of nipping over to Jersey to spend some of his ill-gotten gains. So then I thought, well, suppose he'd been due to go that night and then the fog had stopped him?'

'And then he'd gone back home and found his wife entertaining Nick Wyatt . . . ?' said Jill, anticipating him.

'That's what I think, yes. See, his wife was quite young, a lot younger than Charlie. I think she might well have had an eye for Nick, 'specially if she was finding Charlie a bit of a bore with his being pissed out of his head half the time.'

'You've seen his wife, have you?'

'Yes, I saw her one day at the fairground. Blonde piece . . .' He corrected himself. 'Sorry. Blonde lady. Very expensive-looking.'

'So she married Charlie Monroe for his money, then started looking around for boyfriends.'

Harry shrugged. 'It wouldn't be the first time. And look at it from Nick's point of view. She'd be in a different league to the normal sort of scrubbers . . . sorry, young ladies . . . that he was used to meeting.'

'Well, I'm sure they weren't all young ladies,' she said mischievously. 'I'm sure he met some scrubbers as well.'

'Well, whatever they were, Mrs Charlie Monroe was in a different league. Older, classier, had a flat in London . . .'

'But also had a husband who'd kill him when he found out,' Jill reminded him.

'Well, sure', admitted Harry. 'But perhaps that gave her an appeal of a sort. You know what I mean? The feeling it was dangerous. A sort of aphrodisiac to some people, isn't it?'

'Not to me,' she said with a small shudder, and he knew she was thinking of Greg.

183

'No, but it might have been to him. To a young lad like that, who would never have believed he was going to get caught anyway.'

'Until he was,' she said quietly.

Harry nodded. 'Charlie had his trip to Jersey all planned. His missus had let Nick know, so he'd arranged to have his night off. Come half-six, he leaves me and old Reg at the arcade and sets off for a night of passion.'

'Then the fog comes down.'

'Unfortunately, yes. Which means that you arrive late on your train and Charlie's plane to Jersey never takes off at all.'

She gave a wry smile, understanding at last. 'Which is why we had to go to the airport. To find whether the flight to Jersey that night had been cancelled?'

He nodded. 'Sorry I had to keep you in the dark.'

'So you should be. But you found what you wanted?'

'Oh yes. Not only did they tell me that the flight had been cancelled but also that Charlie Monroe had had a seat booked on it, for which I was very grateful.' He grimaced as he was reminded of the continuing ache from his ankles and added, 'Mind, I wouldn't have been quite so grateful if I'd known that the man I was talking to was then going to get on the phone and tip Charlie off that I'd been asking about him.'

'I suppose he was only doing his job. You must have seemed a bit suspicious. Next time you must trust me more and then I'll ask the questions.'

'I'll remember that. Anyway, do you want to hear the rest of it?'

'What I want to hear first,' she said, 'is why you didn't go and tell the police all this.'

He hesitated. There'd been reasons, of course. He'd had no real evidence and so had gone in search of the murder weapon that would provide it. He'd owed it to Nick, the young man who'd befriended him, to avenge the shameful way in which his life had been brought to its end. Other reasons too. Like the possibility, which Jill herself had pointed out, that he might yet frustrate Greg's attempts to discredit him in print by coming out of this whole sordid business smelling of roses. And something more basic as well: his wish to sort out Charlie Monroe personally as repayment for the dressing-down Charlie had given him outside the crematorium. Plenty of reasons for not going to the police.

'I didn't have any evidence,' he said shortly, choosing the simplest.

'And do you now?'

'Well, yes. The gun.'

'Will that be enough?'

'It'd better be. I'm not going back looking for more.' Then, more seriously, he added, 'There's the wife as well, don't forget. She's still up there in Salmon Gardens. They can always go and have a talk to her.'

Jill nodded. 'And so Charlie Monroe found his flight had been cancelled and went back home . . .' she said slowly, wanting it all spelled out.

'Yes.'

'. . . and found Nick Wyatt in bed with his wife.'

'Yes.'

'Which he didn't like.'

'I'm sure he didn't.'

'And so he pulled out a gun and shot him.'

'Yes. Perhaps he took him for a walk along the promenade first. Perhaps he brought him back to the fairground, there's no telling. But sooner or later he shot him, yes.'

'Then went back and beat up his wife.'

'Looks like it,' agreed Harry. 'Gave her a couple of black eyes, then shunted her off to London where he knew she'd stay well hidden 'cause she wouldn't want anybody to see her in that state anyway.'

'Silly bitch,' said Jill.

'She was probably scared to death of him,' said Harry, more willing to forgive now it was all over. 'Probably thought he was going to do to her what he'd just done to Nick.'

185

'And do you think she'll tell what she knows to the police?'

Harry shrugged. 'Now she knows Charlie's out of harm's way, I think there's every chance she might, yes.'

Neither of Harry's ankles was broken though both were diagnosed as severely strained and were strapped up before he left Casualty. Next morning they took a taxi to the station, saying goodbye to Floribunda and Mrs Melling and catching a last glimpse of the Winter Gardens. They caught the train and returned to London, feeling odd at returning to a home that was still strange to both of them and smelling of paint.

Mrs Monroe's story was indeed told, and at some length, not only to the police but to the world at large. The Sunday morning after Charlie had been sentenced to twenty years for the murder of Nick Wyatt, Jill returned from the newsagent's, waving a copy of the *News of the World*.

'Look at this!'

'You don't normally get that. What happened to *The Observer*?'

'Never mind. Just read it.'

He did. 'My Life with Killer Husband. By Christine Monroe.'

'And look who's written it for her,' prompted Jill eagerly.

He looked and saw on the next line: 'As told to Greg Philips.'

'And now look on the next page.'

He did as she instructed and saw a photograph of himself, coming down the steps of the police-station, with the blue lamp saying 'POLICE' just over his head. The caption beneath read: 'Private investigator Harry Sommers who helped bring a murderer to justice.'

'You're a hero,' said Jill.

'Well, I don't know about that,' said Harry, feeling pleased, 'but at least I avoided being the villain of the piece.'

They read the article together. It told how Charlie Monroe, fairground-owner and south coast entrepreneur, had taken a shine to young Christine, who was appearing in a summer show as magician's assistant. (See accompanying photograph.) Only after their marriage did she learn the truth about her husband's character, his moods of sudden anger from which she never felt safe. Her relationship with Nick was lightly touched on: he was the Prince Charming, in whose company she felt again the zest for living now otherwise lost.

The final part of the article described the night of the murder and was in line with the version of events already guessed at by Harry.

Charlie had indeed planned a trip to Jersey until, frustrated by the weather, he'd returned home. His already foul mood wasn't improved by what he found there. He'd taken Nick from the house and down to the sea's edge where he'd executed him, leaving the tide to do the rest. Meanwhile Christine, locked in her room and fearing that her own execution was about to follow, made a half-hearted attempt at cutting her wrists with a nail-file. Death, however, was to evade her. Charlie returned, knocked her about a bit, then sent her off to London till everything had blown over and the swelling around her eyes gone down. It was an opportunity to do some shopping and consider her next step. She had just made up her mind to go to the police when news of Charlie's arrest reached her.

'And pigs may fly,' observed Jill, coming to the end of the article.

'You might give her the benefit of the doubt,' objected Harry with a smile.

'I don't doubt for one minute that she'd have kept her mouth shut about her murderous husband for just as long as it suited her.'

The next day was a tedious one of surveillance and process-serving. It was late autumn, the leaves had fallen and there was a new chill to the air. It was a relief to get back to the flat. Jill was sitting before the fire marking papers and looked up to receive his kiss.

'Guess who phoned,' she said quietly.

'Who?'

'Greg.' Then quickly, before he could become angry: 'It's all right. He wanted to apologise.'

'For what?' said Harry, still suspicious.

'Well, more or less for everything I think.' To his surprise she gave a sudden, broad grin. 'Especially for all those threats he made about you.'

'Good of him.'

'Yes.'

'So what's so funny?'

'He's in love.'

'Really?'

'And they're going to get married as soon as her divorce comes through.'

Harry stared at her, slow to guess, and then finally realising. 'You mean Charlie Monroe's . . . ?'

'Yes!'

'He's going to marry her?'

'Definitely. He says he's never been so happy. And it makes him realise how badly he's behaved towards me. And towards you. And so he wants to apologise.'

Harry smiled and then began to laugh too, infected by her mirth and their shared relief that the shadow of the unforgiving ex-husband had at last been lifted. And for him to be marrying Christine Monroe, ex-wife of Killer Husband . . . well, the least you could do was wish him luck.

'We could always make it a double wedding,' said Harry when they'd both got over their amusement.

She looked at him. 'Oh yes?'

Clearly she didn't know whether he was serious. Nor did he. Had he just proposed?

'Just a joke,' he said, retreating. 'Unless you really want to.'

'I think I'd rather wait, if you wouldn't mind,' she said, treading carefully.

'I don't mind at all. So long as you won't mind if I ask you again some time.'

'I'll be very disappointed if you don't,' she said.